KIDNAPPED

JAMES PATTERSON is one of the best-known and biggest-selling writers of all time. His books have sold in excess of 325 million copies worldwide and he has been the most borrowed author in UK libraries for the past nine years in a row. He is the author of some of the most popular series of the past two decades – the Alex Cross, Women's Murder Club, Detective Michael Bennett and Private novels – and he has written many other number one bestsellers including romance novels and stand-alone thrillers.

James is passionate about encouraging children to read. Inspired by his own son who was a reluctant reader, he also writes a range of books for young readers including the Middle School, I Funny, Treasure Hunters, House of Robots, Confessions and Maximum Ride series. James is the proud sponsor of the World Book Day Award and has donated millions in grants to independent bookshops. He lives in Florida with his wife and son.

BOOK**SHOTS**

STORIES AT THE SPEED OF LIFE

What you are holding in your hands right now is no ordinary book, it's a BookShot.

BookShots are page-turning stories by James Patterson and other writers that can be read in one sitting.

Each and every one is fast-paced, 100% story-driven; a shot of pure entertainment guaranteed to satisfy.

Available as new, compact paperbacks, ebooks and audio, everywhere books are sold.

BookShots – the ultimate form of storytelling. From the ultimate storyteller.

KIDNAPPED

JAMES
PATTERSON

WITH *ROBERT GOLD*

BOOK**SHOTS**

3 5 7 9 10 8 6 4 2

BookShots

20 Vauxhall Bridge Road
London SW1V 2SA

BookShots is part of the Penguin Random House
group of companies whose addresses can be found at
global.penguinrandomhouse.com

Penguin
Random House
UK

First published by BookShots in 2016

www.penguin.co.uk

A CIP catalogue record for this book is available
from the British Library.

ISBN 9781786530783

Typeset in Garamond Premier Pro font 12/16.5 pt in
India by Thomson Digital Pvt Ltd, Noida Delhi

Printed and bound in Great Britain by Clays Ltd, St Ives Plc

KIDNAPPED

PART 1

23 December

CHAPTER 1

Chicago, Illinois

SNOW WAS FALLING AND the airport road snarled as Jon Roscoe sat cramped in the rear of a Chicago cab. As the car slowly made its way into the city's O'Hare Airport, Roscoe's mind drifted while he gazed through the window at the wintery scene. Imagining the delight his twin daughters would find in the falling flakes, his own heart sank as the traffic ground almost to a halt. All he wanted was to be back home in London with his family.

His car crawled forward in front of terminal buildings and as it did so, Roscoe's attention was drawn to a news story running on the in-cab TV.

'This is Katie Coakley from outside the Cook County Criminal Courthouse,' began the reporter, 'where late last night the manslaughter trial of Matteo Ginevra, son of multimillionaire construction magnate Enzo Ginevra, collapsed sensationally after lead prosecution witness Jerry Davis, a former employee of Tribeca Luxury Hotels, recanted his earlier evidence.

'Davis had previously testified to the Chicago PD to witnessing Matteo Ginevra force two construction workers to ride unsecured on a steel girder, as it was hoisted over fifty floors during the building of the Chicago Tribeca Luxury Hotel. Davis had also testified to Ginevra's appearing intoxicated by liquor while on the construction site.

'Yesterday evening he amended his evidence, stating Matteo Ginevra had attempted to prevent the two construction workers climbing aboard the girder. Both men were killed when the crane jammed and they fell fifty floors to the ground. Now back to the studio.'

Roscoe thumped his hand against the screen of the in-car TV.

Four days wasted in Chicago waiting to testify against Matteo Ginevra had been bad enough, but more than this he was incensed at the thought of a guilty man going free.

Jerry Davis was the third, and most crucial, of the prosecution witnesses to recant their evidence. Roscoe was in no doubt all three had been bought off – and that the Ginevra family fortune had cast a long shadow over the trial.

Two years earlier, as the recently appointed global head of security for Tribeca Luxury Hotels, a chain of the twenty-eight most exclusive hotels across the world, Roscoe had been in Chicago as a member of the team charged with developing the latest addition to the group's luxury portfolio.

With the hotel under construction in the city's downtown district, Roscoe had been responsible for the security structure in and around the hotel's core. Regularly home to some of the world's most powerful and influential people, all Tribeca Luxury Hotels were built with a security foundation that offered the greatest possible level of resistance to the terror threats in existence across the modern world.

That afternoon, as he walked from the hotel along the banks of the Chicago River, Roscoe had seen Matteo Ginevra drinking heavily in one of the newly opened riverside bars. Knowing Ginevra was heading up the Tribeca construction team, Roscoe had felt uncomfortable. But, telling himself Ginevra was the son of Enzo Ginevra and that the Ginevra Construction Group was one of the biggest global partners of Tribeca Luxury Hotels, he had convinced himself Matteo was finished for the day and walked on.

It was a moment's decision that had stayed with him every day for the next two years.

While Roscoe had sat and eaten lunch by the river, an intoxicated Ginevra had returned to the construction site. Surrounded by his entourage, he had started to goad two of the men working on the site. Relishing an opportunity to exhibit his power in front of his devotees, Matteo had bullied the two construction workers into riding unsecured up the outside of the new skyscraper.

The scene Roscoe had discovered when he returned an hour later was one he could still see each time he closed his eyes.

The mangled bodies of the two construction workers had lain shattered in pools of their own blood, having plunged over fifty floors onto the newly constructed sun terrace that overlooked the graceful river.

Now, watching the news report, his anger and frustration surfaced once more. In attempting to deliver a hotel that would provide the ultimate in security for its future guests, he had not provided that same security to the men charged with its construction.

He had failed them.

Listening to the end of the news report, he could still hear Matteo's voice from that tragic afternoon: 'Dead Hispanics are nothing more than a cost of doing business in the construction trade,' he had said to Roscoe as he walked away from the scene.

Roscoe wouldn't rest until Matteo Ginevra was behind bars.

CHAPTER 2

WITH THE SNOW STILL falling, Roscoe's cab made its way round to the American Airlines terminal. His attention was drawn to a teenage girl hurtling out of the front of the building. With no regard for her own safety, she ran through the airport traffic, slamming her hand against the hood of Roscoe's car. Roscoe's driver jammed on his brakes and Roscoe was hurled forward against the cab's partition, only his outstretched arm breaking his fall.

And then, almost instantly, the cab was hit from behind. Roscoe was tossed forward, his head crashing into the divide.

'You okay back there?' said the driver as Roscoe, dazed and with a bloodied temple, pulled himself up off the floor.

'Fine,' said Roscoe, wiping away the blood from his forehead. He felt a pain rip through his right shoulder.

'Stupid kid,' said the driver. 'Gonna get herself killed if she don't watch where she's going.'

Roscoe looked out of his window at the girl, who continued to weave erratically through the traffic, now making her way across the elevated airport approach road.

'Cops coming after her,' said the driver. Roscoe turned to see two police officers exit the terminal building in pursuit of the girl. 'Maybe she's one of those Islam terror women, beholden to their menfolk. She can be beholden to me any time she likes,' he added, laughing to himself.

The driver's last comment was lost on Roscoe, who was already opening his door. Car horns blared and frustrated drivers shouted at the stacked-up vehicles around them, as he ducked through the traffic in pursuit of the girl.

'Hold up!' he called as she ran towards the edge of the elevated road. 'Please, wait!' he shouted. He glanced behind to see the two police officers now with their weapons drawn. With more snow now lying on the ground, he saw one of the officers take a Bambie-style slide across the road, his feet suddenly flying above his head. Car horns sounded with greater intensity in apparent celebration of the officer's undignified fall.

The girl was running across the rail track that encircled the airport to ferry passengers from terminal to terminal. Roscoe doubled his pace.

'Stop! Let me help you,' he shouted again.

The girl turned and looked over her shoulder. Roscoe could see genuine fear etched into her young face.

But she did not stop.

Instead he could only watch as the girl climbed the barrier that edged the elevated road so that she was standing precariously on the concrete ledge.

Roscoe slowed to a stop.

The girl was staring down at a hundred-foot drop below.

CHAPTER 3

'COME AWAY FROM THE edge,' Roscoe pleaded, fearful his voice would be drowned out by the deafening engines of a departing plane, soaring above them.

Blinded by the snow, he moved closer. He could just see the girl's bleached-blonde hair, much of it tucked beneath a Chicago Bears cap, contrasting with her dark, Mediterranean skin. She half turned to look at him and he caught sight of the desperation in her deep brown eyes.

Quickly, she turned back and edged forward to the drop.

'Wait!' called Roscoe, pushing his sodden blonde hair back from his forehead. Looking round, he could see the police officers quickly coming up behind him. Knowing they would only succeed in spooking the girl further, he turned and held up his hands, showing them he was unarmed.

The officers slowed and Roscoe turned back to the girl.

'What's your name?' he called to her, realising the need to engage her in conversation. 'Mine's Jon, and I'm starting to wish I'd grabbed my jacket before I ran after you.'

But the girl said nothing. She continued to balance peril-ously on the ledge, refusing to face Roscoe.

'Can we talk inside the terminal?'

She still didn't reply.

'The police are backing away,' he called, turning to the officers and waving his hand back. With the girl standing on the very precipice he shouted again, frantically trying to make himself heard above the noise of another departing plane. 'We really want to help you!' he called. 'Can you take one step towards me?'

The girl didn't move.

Roscoe edged forward until he was standing directly behind her.

'Nobody's going to hurt you,' he said. Car horns started to blare out once again. 'I'm getting real cold out here, so I'm guessing you're not great either.'

'You're bleeding,' she said, suddenly turning towards him.

'Not my day,' he said with a smile.

'Mine neither.' Roscoe could see the tears well in her eyes as she spoke to him.

'Let's not make it any worse,' he said, reaching towards her. 'I can help you.'

The girl shook her head and turned away abruptly.

'Please . . . please let me try,' he called, quickly realising what she was about to do.

'No one can help me,' she cried, before taking a single step forward.

CHAPTER 4

A SEARING PAIN RIPPED through Roscoe's shoulder as he lunged forwards and grabbed hold of the girl. Even at six foot four inches and over two hundred pounds, catching hold of the girl as she was about to fall tore into the shoulder he had jarred when his cab had been hit from behind.

Ignoring the pain and holding on to the girl, he set her down on the ground. Car horns rapidly sounded and voices cheered as watching airport passengers celebrated the rescue.

'Hi,' Roscoe said to the girl, who didn't reach up to his shoulder in height. 'Let's get you inside.'

Feeling her body judder with cold and fright, he continued to hold her close. When she looked up at him he could see she was fighting back tears while she desperately tried to catch her breath.

'You're safe now.' He smiled, and for the first time she smiled shyly back. 'You never did tell me your name.'

'Cal,' she whispered. 'Calpurnia, but everyone calls me Cal.'

'Nice to meet you, Cal,' said Roscoe, starting to walk her back in the direction of the terminal building. Seeing the two police officers approach, he once again raised his arms to show he was no threat. As he did, he noticed his driver taking his bags from the trunk of the car and dumping them on the snow-covered sidewalk.

'Hey!' he shouted. 'What the hell do you think you're doing?'

'We can't all be superheroes, mister. I've got a living to make.'

'Give me one minute and I'll be right over!'

'We can take it from here, sir,' said one of the police officers, placing a hand on Cal's arm.

'I was hoping we might all be able to go inside and talk this through, officer. I'm a retired cop,' Roscoe continued, having served fifteen years as a member of London's Metropolitan Police, 'and I thought I might be able to help get everything straightened out.'

'That won't be necessary, sir. Thank you for your intervention, but we're able to handle things just fine,' said the younger of the two officers, who Roscoe thought must be straight out of the academy.

'I only want to get an idea of what's happened here,' said Roscoe, reluctant to abandon Cal to the two officers. 'All I can see is a frightened teenage girl and two cops pursuing her with their weapons drawn.'

'You should return to your cab now, sir,' said the senior officer. 'A security protocol was breached and we responded accordingly.'

'Waving your weapons at a girl who is then scared for her life? Is that responding accordingly?'

'I'm fine,' whispered Cal.

'Sir,' said the senior officer, stepping towards Roscoe. 'Homeland Security advisory is of a high risk of a terror attack. Now, please step back and return to your vehicle.'

Roscoe knew it was pointless arguing with the officer, however much he wanted to.

'Are you sure you're going to be okay?' he said, turning to Cal. 'At least tell me what made you run.'

'Mister, you going to pay this fare?' shouted Roscoe's driver. 'Clock's still ticking.'

'I got confused in the security check, that's all,' said Cal.

'Please step away now, sir,' said the younger of the two officers, taking hold of Cal's arm.

'You should do what they say,' said Cal, looking up at Roscoe. She reached up and touched his forehead. 'You're still bleeding.'

'Don't worry about me,' he said, still anxious about her as he wiped the blood away.

'Like *now*, mister!' called the driver.

As Roscoe turned, the officers stepped forward and led Cal away.

Another horn blared and Roscoe moved from the road. His eyes still fixed on Cal, he watched her look back at him as she stepped inside the terminal.

The sadness in her eyes was the image he was left with.

CHAPTER 5

FROZEN TO HIS CORE, his cold, wet shirt sticking to his body, Roscoe jogged back to his cab in a desperate attempt to warm himself through. Reaching into his pocket, he pulled out sixty bucks and slapped them into the cabbie's outstretched hand.

'And a Merry Christmas to you,' said Roscoe, dismissing the driver before he picked up his bags from the sidewalk. As he did so, he looked down the passenger drop-off zone to where a young couple were standing arguing while their child sat in a snow-covered buggy. They were impossible to ignore.

He could hear the man scream at his wife to get back inside the cab. Throwing open the door, the man placed his hand on the small of the woman's back and thrust her towards the car. Pushing back on her heels, the woman resisted but, on the slippery sidewalk, it was impossible for her to hold firm. Her feet went from under her and she fell to the ground.

Wanting only to be drinking a hot cup of coffee in the departure lounge, Roscoe still couldn't help but walk down the drop-off zone in the direction of the family. As he did the woman scrambled to her feet and shouted at the man Roscoe assumed to be her husband.

'Brayden and I are going to London and I couldn't care less if you come with us or not,' she said, grabbing hold of her bags and starting to push her by now screaming child in its buggy. Hearing her speak with an English accent, Roscoe thought he recognised her.

'Get back in the cab!' yelled the man.

But Roscoe could see the woman was already making her way towards the terminal building. The man slammed the cab door and started to follow his wife down the snowy walkway.

When she passed directly by Roscoe, her young son still screaming, he again thought he remembered seeing her somewhere before. Was she a friend of his wife, Marika? He didn't think so, and this woman couldn't have been more than twenty-two or -three. He watched as her husband quickly made his way through the snow and snatched the child's buggy from her hands, leaving her to follow, dragging her family's luggage behind her.

Picking up his own bags, Roscoe followed the family inside the terminal. Entering the building, he relished the warmth and pulled open his holdall to find a dry sweater. The cold still coursing through his veins, he ripped off his shirt, rubbed down his hair and wiped away any remaining blood from his face. Appreciative of the one wolf whistle he received from two passing women, he pulled on his favourite sweater and immediately started to feel the benefit.

Having stuffed his wet shirt inside his bag, he found his passport and looked for his check-in counter. Making his way through the concourse to the American Airlines bag drop, he looked ahead to see Cal standing with the two police officers but now joined by a third man.

Roscoe stopped suddenly.

The third man was Matteo Ginevra.

CHAPTER 6

STANDING NO MORE THAN a hundred feet away from him was the man Roscoe had come to Chicago to convict.

It was the first time the two men had come face to face since Matteo Ginevra had walked away from Roscoe with the dead bodies of two construction workers lying on the newly built riverside terrace, more than two years earlier.

That afternoon Roscoe had smelt the alcohol on Ginevra's breath as he'd dismissed the deaths of the two Hispanic construction workers as a cost of business. Ginevra's only concern had been the bonus payments his father's company might miss if there was a delay in the handover of the building.

Locking eyes with him now, Roscoe realised how much he hated the man.

Refusing to break eye contact, he moved towards Ginevra, ready for the confrontation he believed should have occurred in the Chicago courthouse.

Matteo Ginevra had changed little in the intervening years. His jet-black hair, matched in colour by his designer clothes, was still slicked back from his mottled face – a face that had seen every aspect of life in its twenty-five years.

Ginevra stood motionless, Cal and the two police officers by his side. As Roscoe approached, Cal lifted her head from beneath her tightly fitting baseball cap and quietly shook her head, as though pleading with him to stay away.

Roscoe stopped.

Matteo Ginevra grinned at him, putting his arm possessively around Cal's shoulders.

The hectic buzz of the airport continued around him as Roscoe watched Ginevra lead Cal away, the two police officers following. As Matteo steered her through the security check, Roscoe found himself hoping Cal would again turn her head towards him.

But this time she didn't.

Roscoe thought of the fear that had made Cal run out of the airport and threaten to take her own life. He knew the horror Ginevra was capable of and he was convinced the desperation he had seen in Cal's eyes was a desperation created by Ginevra.

The sound of a loud sob suddenly cut through Roscoe's thoughts.

He looked across the terminal to see the man he had watched outside now sitting on a bench, tightly holding his young son in his arms. Before him stood his wife, her thin, pale face turned scarlet as tears streaked down her cheeks.

Passengers lining up to check their bags stood and stared at the couple, allowing them to provide a distraction from the monotony of waiting in long holiday airport lines. As he walked towards them, Roscoe could see the woman plead with her husband to hand over their son, but him refusing.

'Hello,' he said to the woman as the man got to his feet and put his son into his buggy. 'I was thinking that maybe I can help you guys here. I know how stressful travelling at this time of year can be, especially with a little one in tow.'

'I'm sorry, we're moving on,' said the woman, wiping her eyes. 'Wyatt, please, let's just go.'

Her husband looked up at her as he tightened the straps around his son. 'Surely you never thought I'd let you go without me?' he said to his wife, ignoring Roscoe.

Roscoe simply stepped in front of the child's buggy. 'Don't I know you from somewhere?' he asked.

'Not us,' said the man, trying to move around Roscoe's imposing frame. 'Emily, we've got a plane to catch.'

'Emily?' said Roscoe. 'Emily Montgomerie? Your mother lives in the house next door to my wife's parents, doesn't she?'

He watched the relief flood across the woman's face.

'Of course, you're Marika's husband. I'm Emily Lee now. This is my husband, Wyatt. Wyatt, Marika's parents live next door to my mother in St Barnham. You won't believe it but that's where we're heading; we must go and say hi to them on this trip. We should do that, shouldn't we, Wyatt?' she said, looking at him. 'Great to see you,' she continued, turning back to Roscoe, 'it really is. Isn't it funny how you can run into people anywhere in the world? Here we are such a long way from London and St Barnham and we bump into you! And I'm so sorry, I really am, but you're going to have to remind me of your name.'

'Jon – Jon Roscoe.'

'Of course, Jon, yes, now I remember. Wyatt, this is Jon,' Emily said to her husband as he took a step back, seemingly riled by Roscoe's intervention. 'Wyatt, I think you met Marika last time we were over, or at the very least we said hello over the garden wall. You remember. Wyatt?'

'How the hell would I remember?' said Wyatt, gripping hold of the handles on his child's buggy. 'That was nearly three years ago. Brayden wasn't even born.'

'No, you're right, of course you are, I'm sorry. I was about four months pregnant at the time. How is Marika, though? And your girls must be getting older.'

'Seven, almost eight,' said Roscoe. 'They're all great, the girls are very excited about Christmas. Marika and I are separated but we're all going to be together for the holidays.'

'I'm sorry to hear that but, yes, we can't wait to be back home for the holidays. I can't anyway,' she said, looking to her husband. 'It's much harder for Wyatt to be away from his family, I can understand that, and he doesn't really know anyone in London.'

'We aren't going anywhere if we don't catch this flight,' said Wyatt, the vein in his neck visible as he spoke.

'Yes, sorry, Wyatt, you're right,' said Emily, collecting up all of the family's baggage once more. 'Perhaps we'll see you in St Barnham? Give my love to Marika and say hi to the girls.'

She started to move down the airport concourse but Roscoe remained stationary in front of her child's buggy. Almost imperceptibly he leant towards Wyatt.

'Travelling at Christmas can be very stressful,' he said quietly. 'My advice is to take a deep breath, move three steps back and let the calm wash all over you.'

Wyatt said nothing.

Roscoe leant further into the man. 'You hear what I'm saying?'

Wyatt Lee nodded and Roscoe slowly stepped aside.

'Great to see you,' called Emily as her husband moved past Roscoe and quickly caught up with her.

Standing by the bench, Roscoe watched as Emily soon struggled to keep pace, almost running at Wyatt's side. Wyatt reached down as if to take hold of his wife's hand.

Instead he gripped her wrist.

CHAPTER 7

THE SOUND OF A hundred-strong gospel choir, dressed head to toe in red and white robes, filled the airport concourse when Roscoe exited the security check and started to make his way towards his departure gate. Stopping for a moment to appreciate the choir's rendition of 'I'll Be Home for Christmas', he thought of his own family arriving in London from their home in Edinburgh and for the first time he looked forward to the holiday season.

For Roscoe, Christmas had long since become a time of mixed emotions. Fourteen years earlier his younger sister, Amanda, had been brutally attacked only two days before Christmas. A few days later, he had had to make the unbearable decision to disconnect her life support.

As a young man of only twenty-two, he had adopted Amanda's only child, Martin, and ever since had endeavoured to be the best possible father to him. When Roscoe had celebrated the birth of his own twin daughters seven years later,

Martin had remained a fundamental and much-loved part of the Roscoe family.

For all children Christmas is a magical time and the Roscoe children were no exception. He thought of the joy of having all his family together once again for the Christmas holiday, even if for him and Martin it was still a time to remember their saddest days.

Reaching into his pocket, he took out his last remaining dollar bills and threw them into the red collection bucket held by a small child at the front of the choir. Smiling at the little girl, he stepped away, the festive music still ringing in his ears.

'Very generous of you,' said Matteo Ginevra, coming up alongside him. 'Always good to support charitable efforts at this time of year, however meagre your contribution.' He took a roll of notes from the pocket of his leather jacket, peeled off a hundred-dollar bill and dropped it in the bucket. The girl's eyes opened wide when she saw the money, and Matteo said, 'Happy holidays from the Ginevra family.'

Ignoring him, Roscoe walked down the long concourse but Matteo remained in step beside him.

'What do you want?' said Roscoe.

'To wish you and your family all the best for the holidays,' replied Matteo. 'And to say how sorry I am that your trip to Chicago was such a wasted one.'

'There'll be another trial,' said Roscoe.

'It's over – let it go. Jerry Davis has moved to a new luxury condo in Florida – fourteenth floor, looking over a white sandy beach, truly living the high life. He won't want to come back to windy old Chicago.'

Roscoe kept walking.

'That makes you the last man standing,' said Ginevra. 'Which is never going to be enough to build a case on. You should go home and enjoy some time with that beautiful young family of yours.'

Roscoe stopped. 'What do you know about my family?'

'Only that they're looking forward to a nice quiet Christmas with their papa, just like I am. You can't beat being with family at Christmas.'

'Enjoy it while you can,' said Roscoe, dropping his voice. 'I saw you drunk that afternoon. You forced those men onto that girder and then laughed when they clung for their lives.'

'You're mistaken. If only you'd been there, you'd have heard how hard I tried to stop them.'

Roscoe squared up to Ginevra.

'Go on,' said Ginevra, 'throw a punch – you know you want to. With all these witnesses, perhaps the choir could sing at your trial.'

Roscoe balled his fist but held it against his chest.

'Lost your nerve?' said Ginevra. 'Stay away from me, Roscoe, and keep away from my family.'

'Your family?' said Roscoe.

Ginevra pointed across the terminal to where Cal was standing, and smiled. 'On our way to London to enjoy the delights of the Tribeca Luxury Hotel. Spending Christmas with our papa – just my baby sister and me.'

CHAPTER 8

HANDING HIS CREDIT CARD to the assistant in the final airport gift shop before he reached his departure gate, Roscoe had been unable to resist one last purchase. Wandering around the store, while the assistant gift-wrapped two plush Chicago Cubs brown bears, he'd imagined how excited his young daughters would be with only two more nights' sleep until Christmas.

He looked forward to the time they would spend together as a family over the holiday, but wished Marika and his daughters were returning to the house in the London area of Brixton where they had lived for the past seven years.

He thought of the day he and Marika had brought their daughters, Lauren and Aimee, home from the hospital for the very first time. Waiting on the step outside their house had been Martin, along with his grandmother Jessie. As they all went inside the house, Roscoe had closed the big front door behind them and had felt they were safe in a place that would be their home for ever.

Instead, this Christmas, Marika and his daughters would be staying with her parents in the village of St Barnham. It was only twenty minutes' drive away from Brixton, but for Roscoe it was a distance so great he wondered if it would ever be breached.

He had now been separated from Marika for almost a year. Twelve months earlier he had taken his family to stay in Edinburgh for the grand opening of the Tribeca Luxury Hotel. At the time, he had felt his marriage was strained but had failed to realise how far Marika's life had already separated from his.

After three weeks in Edinburgh, Marika had announced she planned to remain in the city and that their girls would stay with her. Roscoe had let himself become consumed in his work and in doing so he had let her drift away from him. Now, collecting the gift bag from the assistant, he hoped this Christmas would be the start of bringing his wife and family home.

By the time he reached the departure gate for his overnight journey back to London, his flight had already been called. He joined the line for a final security check before handing his boarding pass to the waiting attendant. Ahead of him, he saw Emily and Wyatt Lee standing together in silence. And then bypassing those around them, as they headed to the first-class cabin, came Matteo and Cal Ginevra.

Never able to sleep on long flights, Roscoe planned to catch up on a couple of movies on his journey home. Finding his seat, he opened the overhead storage to load in the assortment of gifts he was taking back for his family. With space at a premium, he slipped one bag inside another. As he did so he noticed a single sheet of paper folded inside one of his bags.

Taking his seat, he opened the paper up and, with a shudder running down his spine, he read the handwritten message:

'PLEASE HELP BEFORE HE KILLS ME.'

PART 2

Christmas Eve

CHAPTER 9

St Barnham, London

MARIKA ROSCOE LAY IN her bed and stared into the darkness. She had lain for over an hour, hoping sleep would overtake her, but her mind refused to rest. Looking at the clock beside her, she saw the time had ticked past 1 a.m. and yet she felt as awake as she had when she'd said goodnight to her parents a little after eleven.

Being back in her parents' house wasn't easy.

She had been raised in a home that had found a balance between traditional Japanese culture and modern living in a city as metropolitan as London. Her parents had supported her through university and medical school, always encouraging her to find her own strong path in life.

The day she had married Jon, nine years earlier, had been one of the most wonderful days of her life – and the happiest of theirs.

She loved her parents dearly and they had never ceased to want the very best for her. And in their eyes that meant a happy marriage to Jon. They now found it impossible to accept or understand that she and Jon were separated; at times she found it almost impossible to understand herself.

In the years they had built their family together, never had she imagined that one day she and Jon would be apart. She had always looked upon herself as one of the lucky ones. While her friends might have complained about their husbands or their lack of a career, Marika had felt she had it all. She had treasured her life as a family doctor in London and had loved Jon in a way she had never thought possible.

But over time, Jon and the life he led had become increasingly difficult. His work took him away for days or even weeks at a time. He couldn't tell her when he would be home and, worse than that, she knew he never backed away when his life was in danger. Eventually she'd told herself she couldn't keep living that way.

With her daughters growing older she had known she needed to provide stability in their lives. Jon loved his job and while she'd never wanted to take that away from him, she hadn't been able to live night after night waiting to hear from him and hoping he would return home safely. Her daughters needed more than that. She needed more than that.

Marika turned over in her bed and found herself watching the digital numbers on the clock as the minutes slowly ticked by. She counted sixty seconds for each minute and on her eleventh attempt found she was as accurate in counting a minute as the red-numbered clock. Finally, at one forty, she told herself that lying in bed counting seconds was ridiculous and she pushed back her covers.

She walked to the window and cracked open the blinds. Looking out upon the picturesque village of St Barnham, she realised how much she loved her childhood home. Standing tall in the centre of the village was a Christmas tree illuminated by lights, casting a warm glow across the charming scene. The Victorian street lamps threw light across each of the red-brick homes, and the ancient church by the side of the village pond – where records dated back to the thirteenth century – still reminded her of her childhood singing in the choir.

As a white frost laid itself upon the stone sidewalks, Marika treasured the scene. A shooting star raced across the clear night sky and she made a wish that her own daughters would grow up with the same cherished memories of their home – even if their home was four hundred miles away in the Scottish city of Edinburgh.

About to pull the blinds back down, she spotted a figure crouching in the garden of the neighbouring house. She watched as the shape moved through the shadows, seeming to squat beside the gold Jaguar convertible belonging to Dame Annabel Montgomerie. Marika edged up the blinds a little further and as she did the darkly dressed figure moved quickly from the front of the Montgomerie house, around the pond and across to the opposite side of the village, where it disappeared into the night.

Marika Roscoe wasn't the only inhabitant of the village of St Barnham unable to sleep.

As he walked into his bedroom and peered out through the small window, Julian Templeton was feeling a great sense of anticipation. Today he was preparing for the arrival of a very special guest.

Later, he would walk through the crowded village and observe its inhabitants making rash last-minute Christmas decisions. He never made any rash decisions; for him preparation was everything. He had made a list of required purchases and he would follow it precisely. When he passed the coffee shop, the woman who served him each morning would wave in expectation of his entrance. Today he would move quickly by, holding up his shopping basket to indicate there was much to be done. He knew nothing must appear out of the ordinary.

Everyone would be planning their celebrations. But not him; he had his own festivities to plan. He mustn't let his excitement distract him.

Everything had to be perfect for the arrival of his little guest.

CHAPTER 10

THIRTY-EIGHT THOUSAND FEET ABOVE the Atlantic, Jon Roscoe sat upright in his chair in the darkened aircraft cabin. All around him his fellow passengers slept. But with his mind racing around the Ginevra family, he hadn't relaxed for a single moment since leaving Chicago. Even the action in the latest Hollywood blockbuster had failed to distract him.

Leaning forward, he reached for the anonymous note left inside his bag at O'Hare Airport. The handwritten note simply read: 'PLEASE HELP BEFORE HE KILLS ME.' He had read it over and over since leaving the United States. He couldn't help but think of the desperate look on Cal's face, as she was led away first by the two Chicago police officers and then by her brother Matteo.

Roscoe knew exactly what Ginevra was capable of. He had seen the consequences of the man's sadistic behaviour with his own eyes. Roscoe was certain that Ginevra belonged behind bars and was determined he would be the one to put him there.

But what, he wondered, had made Cal so fearful? Was her brother threatening her? Was that why she had run? Roscoe remembered the petrified look on her face as she'd stood at the edge of the airport road, ready to jump the hundred feet to her death. What would have happened if he hadn't been there?

Closing his eyes, he could still see the terror in hers.

He had to talk to her.

Lying awake throughout the flight, he had waited for his opportunity to speak with her – and now his opportunity had come. Through the semi-darkness, he watched as she walked silently down the aisle, gently brushing against him as she passed his seat and continued towards the bathroom.

Ignoring the pain that shot through his shoulder as he pushed himself up, he slipped the note into his back pocket and followed her down the aisle.

Looking ahead, he could see she had stopped outside the bathroom. Aware her brother might see them both, he glanced back down the aisle but the cabin remained silent. He stepped forward until he was standing directly behind her.

'I can help you,' he said, 'but I need you to tell me how.'

Cal was silent.

'I know you're frightened,' he said, leaning forward to whisper in her ear, 'but I can't help you unless you tell me more.'

'I want you to,' she said, turning to look at him in the shallow light, her arresting eyes looking directly into his. Seeing her again, he realised she must be around seventeen or eighteen years old. 'Come in here.'

She opened the bathroom door.

'I can't do that,' said Roscoe, surprised. 'You know that.'

As the light from inside the bathroom lit up Cal's face, Roscoe could see tears start to well in her eyes. Dropping her head and turning away, she stepped inside the tiny space.

Roscoe hesitated. He thought of the horror Matteo Ginevra had inflicted upon the two construction workers and their families. He knew the evil the man was capable of. Could Cal offer a way of ensnaring him?

After a moment, he followed her into the cramped room and she locked the door behind them.

CHAPTER 11

THE METALLIC SCREAM OF an ear-piercing alarm smashed through the night-time silence in the village of St Barnham. Back in bed, Marika Roscoe was instantly awake and, quickly looking at her clock, she saw time had ticked forward to 4 a.m. The ferocity of the alarm, coming from the neighbouring Montgomerie house, sent a pulse drumming through her head.

Going straight to the window of her room, she opened the blinds once more and discovered the lights inside the Montgomerie house were fully illuminated. But within seconds the alarm was extinguished and the village returned to its silent slumber. As it did, Marika watched Dame Annabel Montgomerie emerge from the front of her home and stand alone in her garden.

Grabbing a sweater from beside her bed, Marika slipped on her pumps and headed out of her room. Meeting her mother on the stairs, she asked her to check her daughters were still sleeping before making her way downstairs.

The cold, thin winter air momentarily took her breath away as she stepped outside her parents' house. Hurrying towards the neighbouring garden, she called out to Dame Annabel, 'Is everything okay?'

'I'm so sorry,' replied Annabel as Marika entered her garden. 'Someone has thrown a brick through the glass door at the back of my house. It sent the alarms into an absolute frenzy. It's an occupational hazard, I'm afraid. I'm just so sorry if it has woken you all.'

'Don't worry,' said Marika, reaching for Annabel's arm to reassure her. 'I'm just glad you're okay. It was such a terrifying noise. Who would want to do something like that?'

'Sadly, I'm used to it. With my writings and lectures I've made myself a bit of an easy target, particularly at this time of year. I'm afraid not everybody wants to see someone on television telling them there is no real Christmas.'

A renowned scientist, author and controversial atheist thinker, Dame Annabel Montgomerie was known the world over. Her writings had made her a wealthy woman but her views on religion had turned her into a contentious and sometimes hated figure.

'The police will be here any moment. The alarm registers directly with them and a squad car is sent straight over,' she continued. 'The alarm is so sensitive I end up living in lockdown between the hours of eleven p.m. and seven a.m. Any movement downstairs and the alarm is triggered. It is almost always nothing but I suppose it's better to be safe than sorry.'

Marika smiled, but she wondered if voicing such strident views was worth the price Dame Annabel paid in sacrifices to her liberty.

And was a brick smashing into your home in the dead of night really nothing?

Dame Annabel steadfastly refused her offer of a cup of tea. Marika saw a police car enter the far end of the village. Once again Dame Annabel assured her she would be fine, so Marika said goodnight and turned to leave.

Walking back past the vintage E-Type Jaguar, parked proudly in the driveway, Marika noticed the damage she had failed to see when she'd hurriedly made her way into the garden. Calling Annabel across, the two women stood by the car, illuminated by the lights from the village Christmas tree.

Sprayed in red paint across its length were the words: 'JESUS LIVES. YOU DIE'.

CHAPTER 12

INSIDE THE CRAMPED AIRPLANE bathroom Roscoe felt trapped.

He was beginning to doubt his decision to follow Cal in, but, as her intense, dark eyes stared up at him, he remembered there were no depths to which her brother would not sink. He was determined he would be the one to provide her with the help she needed – even if he didn't yet know how.

'What made you so frightened at the airport, Cal?' asked Roscoe.

Cal laced her fingers through Roscoe's. 'Do you really think Matteo was guilty of killing those men?' she asked. 'You were meant to testify against him, weren't you?'

'I don't think he's guilty – I *know* he's guilty,' replied Roscoe. 'I saw the men's bodies after they'd fallen. I know what it's done to their families. They'll never recover. Is that what this is about? You have to tell me.'

But Cal had turned away.

'You do know something, don't you?'

'No,' said Cal. 'I don't know anything.' She sighed. 'Matteo is a boy wanting to be the big man. He wants to be the papa of the family. Maybe one day he will be.'

'Not if I can help it,' said Roscoe. 'He doesn't belong in any kind of business. He belongs in a jail cell.'

'I don't know, perhaps he does,' said Cal, turning back to look at Roscoe. 'I'm frightened.'

'Why?' he asked.

'I don't want to go to London, don't want to see my father, my stepmother or their spoilt child.'

'Tell me why not?' For a moment Roscoe wondered if Cal was the spoilt child and he pulled his hand away. 'Who are you scared of? Your father? Your stepmother? You have to tell me or I can't help you.'

'Nobody can help me.'

Roscoe was becoming frustrated. He turned to leave.

'I would've jumped if it hadn't been for you,' she said, with greater urgency. 'You saved my life once. Would you do it again?'

'You're playing games with me, Cal,' said Roscoe, turning back to face her. 'I need you to tell me what you're scared of, or you're right: I can't help you.'

Cal dropped her head into her hands. 'If I do I'm afraid of what he'll do to me.'

Roscoe reached for her hand. 'What will he do?'

'I'm afraid he'll kill me.'

CHAPTER 13

WALKING DOWN THE STAIRS of her parents' home soon after eight o'clock on the morning of Christmas Eve, Marika Roscoe felt drained after her broken sleep during the night.

She entered the kitchen and found her daughters, Aimee and Lauren, already eating breakfast with their grandmother Umi. Kissing both girls on the cheek, she was pleased to hear neither of them had been woken by the alarm.

'That horrendous noise cuts through me every time it goes off,' said her mother. Marika crossed the kitchen and poured herself a mug of coffee from the freshly brewed pot. 'I simply don't understand why it has to be so loud. It seems pointless to me.'

'I guess they hope it might scare someone away.'

'Perhaps so. But as far as I can make out, half the time it goes off it's a false alarm.' Umi busied herself at the sink. 'Did they catch anyone this time?'

'I don't think so. I left Annabel with the police,' replied Marika. 'But I know I wouldn't want my door smashed through in the middle of the night or my car vandalised.'

'Yes, I saw that,' said Umi with greater interest. 'What did the great dame make of that?'

'I'm sure she was scared, Mama,' said Marika, 'although she didn't really show it.'

'She never does,' said her mother. 'She's always so controlled. I do wonder, though, how much she brings it on herself.' She put two slices of toast on the table in front of Marika. 'If I was her I'd think about keeping my mouth shut, especially at this time of year. You'd think she didn't know it was Christmas.'

Marika smiled. 'Everyone is entitled to their views,' she said.

'She's never off the television,' said Umi. 'She was at the Barbican giving a lecture yesterday evening and from what I understand she's on another programme today. It's Christmas Eve. She should be at home. You do know her daughter arrives from America today?'

'I did hear,' said Marika. 'I remember Emily.'

'I thought you'd remember her,' replied Umi, and Marika saw the relish in her mother's face as she began her story. 'She went off to university in America, hailed by her mother as the next great scientist. Instead she dropped out after a year, got herself pregnant and married a real down-and-out with no job and no prospects. She had a little boy and called him Brayden. What kind of name is that?'

Marika sighed. 'As long as they're happy.'

'Well, that's the thing – according to Dame Annabel, they're not.'

'I didn't know Annabel confided in you.'

'Occasionally,' said Umi with a smile. 'Anyway, all I'm saying is she should keep her opinions to herself, and perhaps if she stayed home more her daughter wouldn't have got herself into the mess she's in.'

'Everyone has to work, Mama,' said Marika.

'Call that work? You work; Jon works. She doesn't work. She talks. And a little too much for my liking. But enough about her.' Umi took a seat at the table next to her daughter. 'It's Christmas Eve, a day of great romance.'

'Mama . . .' said Marika, knowing immediately what was coming next.

'In Japan, Christmas Eve is a day of great romance, especially for you young people. A day to dine with your loved one, to make them feel special.'

'I'm glad you still see me as one of the young people. But your point is?'

'You haven't even seen Jon's wonderful new hotel and I hear it has some of the very best restaurants in London. The two of you should have dinner together tonight. Your papa and I can look after the girls.'

'Mama,' said Marika, softening her voice in front of her daughters. 'You know Jon and I are separated.'

'And it breaks my heart every day. You've taken my precious granddaughters four hundred miles to hide away up in Scotland.'

'It's where I work.'

'Don't tell me we don't need doctors here in London. We need one right here in St Barnham. All I see is young mothers walking round the pond with their sickly children. None are so bright and beautiful as my granddaughters.' She paused. 'He is your husband, Marika, the father of your children.'

'Mama, enough,' said Marika, wanting to bring an end to the conversation.

'Okay, no more,' said Umi. 'But I know he still loves you.'

A moment later, Marika's father, Ken, walked into the kitchen and kissed his daughter on the back of her head.

'Papa,' said Marika. 'You've arrived just in time to save me.'

'Don't expect me to save you,' he said with a smile.

'I've already told her we will look after the girls this evening while she and Jon go for dinner,' said Umi, getting to her feet and pouring her husband a mug of coffee.

'But Jon will want to see the girls.'

'He'll want to see his wife as well,' said Ken.

'Papa!'

'What do we know?' said Ken, turning to his wife. 'What possible advice could we give after thirty-eight years of wonderful marriage?'

'I give in,' said Marika, hiding her exasperation with lightness in her voice. 'Jon and I will have dinner together over Christmas, only perhaps not tonight.'

'You promise?' said Umi.

'I promise,' said Marika, thinking of the seven years' bad luck she would suffer for lying to her mother.

CHAPTER 14

NOTWITHSTANDING THE FACT HE hadn't slept for close to twenty-four hours, Roscoe felt surprisingly alert as he travelled from London's Heathrow Airport in the mid-morning holiday traffic. Sitting in the rear of a chauffeur-driven Tribeca Luxury Hotels car, he was delighted to be home. And he knew waiting for him in the village of St Barnham would be his two wonderful daughters along with their mother, whom he still missed every single day.

As the car pulled into the village he spotted his daughters chasing ducks around the ice-covered pond. Leaning forward, he asked the driver to pull over and he quickly made his way across to them. Seeing their father approach, Lauren and Aimee rushed towards him and Roscoe scooped them up, one in each arm, as they hugged him tightly around his neck.

The two girls peppered him with questions, mostly about what gifts he had brought them from America. He told them they would have to wait to see what presents Santa

Claus brought them that night, although if they looked in his bags they might find one or two things they could open now.

Each of the girls gave him one more squeeze before he set them back on the ground and they raced across to rifle through his luggage. As he put Lauren down he flinched, feeling the torn muscles in his shoulder. Looking up, he watched his wife walk towards him, his heart still racing the same way it did the very first time he met her.

'Hello,' said Marika as Roscoe kissed her on the cheek. 'Did I see you wincing?'

'It's nothing, doctor, I promise. You look great,' he said, wanting to reach across and run his hand through her smooth, dark hair.

She pressed her fingers into his damaged shoulder. He flinched again.

'Jon?'

'I had a bit of a bump, nothing serious,' he said, touching the cut on his forehead. 'The ligaments need a couple of days to settle down, that's all.'

'You need to get it looked at,' she said, pulling her coat tight around her.

'The girls seem excited.'

'Very,' she said. 'They can't wait for tomorrow.'

'Neither can I.'

'How was Chicago?'

'Bit of a wasted journey,' said Roscoe. 'The Ginevra trial collapsed. Matteo got to some of the witnesses, I'm sure of it. But he needn't think this is over.' He thought of the tears in Cal's eyes when she had walked away from him on the plane. 'I'll find more evidence.'

Marika took a band from her pocket and tied her hair back. 'Jon, you can't fight every battle.'

'I know he's guilty.'

'Then let somebody else prove it!'

They walked on as Aimee and Lauren discovered the two plush bears along with T-shirts, colouring books and a copy of *How the Grinch Stole Christmas!* They hugged their father again before heading inside to show their grandmother.

'How's it going with Umi?' asked Roscoe.

'You know what my mum's like.'

'She has strong views on many things.'

Marika smiled. 'We had quite a drama here last night – a brick was thrown through a glass door at Dame Annabel's.'

'Not nice,' said Roscoe, 'but I'm guessing it was the usual religious crew?'

'Looks like it,' said Marika. 'Her car was vandalised as well with some pretty nasty graffiti. Funny thing is, I'm sure I saw someone hanging around the car around half past one in the morning, but the alarm wasn't raised until four.'

'Somebody doing a recce?'

'Maybe,' she said.

Roscoe stopped at the gate to his in-laws' garden. 'I want to ask you something before we head inside.'

'Go on,' said Marika hesitantly.

'Have dinner with me tonight, at home, in our house, just you and me.'

'Jon—'

'Please.'

Marika turned and put her hand on Roscoe's arm. 'It's Christmas Eve. I've got so much to do for the girls. Maybe later in the week.'

'I'm going to hold you to that,' he said, trying to hide his disappointment. They watched as a black cab stopped outside the Montgomerie house. 'Looks like Annabel's daughter and her husband.'

'You know them?' asked Marika.

'Let's say we ran into each other at O'Hare. Turned out we were on the same flight.'

As the couple stepped out of the cab, Emily carrying her son Brayden, Roscoe called across to them, 'Hello again.'

'Oh, hi,' said Emily. 'Small world. You made it back okay?'

Roscoe nodded.

'So this is Brayden,' Marika said, walking across to them. 'How old is he now?'

'Coming up to three. Wyatt, this is Marika, and you know Jon.' Wyatt raised his eyebrows in acknowledgement. 'It's Brayden's first visit to London so we're all very excited.'

'Too right it's his first visit,' said Wyatt. 'Cost of the flights alone, I could've bought a new car.'

'My mum helped out,' said Emily.

'That's nice of her,' said Marika.

'If Dame Annie wants to throw some charity my way I'm not going to say no, am I? Looking at this place again, it's clear she's not short of cash.' Wyatt laughed bitterly, and Roscoe could see the anger in him that was never far from the surface. 'She didn't want me here in the first place – tried not to include me in the family reunion. Well, ho, ho, ho, here I am!'

'I'm sure she'll be delighted to have all her family here at Christmas,' said Marika.

'I'm not sure Christmas is a big thing for the dame,' said Wyatt. 'And it isn't as if she hasn't been over enough times to see us. Not that she ever stays anywhere nearby – more of an uptown gal.'

'We only have a small apartment,' said Emily.

Wyatt laughed. 'Apartment? It's one room in a basement.'

'One day we'll have more, honey.'

'Sure, when the dame is dead,' said Wyatt, 'and we get our hands on this place.'

*

Standing at his window, under the guise of decorating his Christmas tree, Julian Templeton watched the new arrivals. From his living room he was able to observe most of the occupants of the village.

Now his final preparations were complete. The room had been readied; the bed had been made. It was little more than cushions and blankets on the floor but they would have to suffice.

His little visitor was in the village.

And Julian was ready for tonight. Christmas Eve. The most exciting night of the year.

CHAPTER 15

DARKNESS HAD FALLEN AND a damp winter cold sat in the air as Roscoe took a cab to the London Tribeca Luxury Hotel. Walking into the foyer in the early evening, he thought how magnificent the building looked. He was awestruck by the glorious Christmas tree, stretching up through the atrium, its brilliant lights throwing sparkle across the marbled entrance.

Open for six months, in the city's Mayfair district, the hotel offered the most exclusive accommodation in London. With lavish suites individually decorated, restaurants serving some of the finest cuisine offered anywhere in England and a heated infinity pool on the fortieth floor providing breathtaking views across the city, the hotel represented the ultimate in luxury.

As global head of security, Roscoe had accountability for each one of the group's twenty-eight hotels around the world but for the first six months of opening he had taken personal responsibility for the London location. The death of the group's chairman, Jackson Harlington, in the days directly before the opening of the London hotel had left him with a challenging six months. Now, with the hotel's reputation fully established and every suite reserved, he was delighted the Christmas holiday was set to be such a resounding success.

Crossing the marbled floor, he spotted Anna Conquest, the hotel's lobby manager. He had worked closely with Anna over the past year, first in Edinburgh and then at the opening of the London hotel. More and more he found himself enjoying the time he spent with her.

'Welcome home,' said Anna as they exchanged a brief kiss.

'Good to be back,' said Roscoe.

'I'm guessing Chicago didn't go quite according to plan.'

'You've heard?' He took a seat on one of the luxurious sofas in the entrance lobby. 'You must have good sources.'

'I don't need sources,' said Anna, perching on the arm of the sofa. 'Matteo Ginevra checked in just before lunch.'

Roscoe said nothing.

'You okay?' she asked, touching his shoulder.

'Fine,' he said. 'I knew he'd be here. Doesn't mean I have to like it. Was his sister with him?'

'Is that Calpurnia?'

'Yes.'

'They're sharing a suite on the twenty-eighth floor,' said Anna. 'Their father, his wife and their little girl, Harper, are in the neighbouring suite. You know, the wife, Kellie, is only twenty-three, twenty-four at the most. She must be younger than Matteo.'

'How did Cal seem?' asked Roscoe.

'Cal?' replied Anna.

'The sister. Everyone calls her Cal.'

'I didn't realise you knew all the family so well,' said Anna. 'She sat across the foyer when they arrived, kept her baseball cap pulled down over her face. I didn't really notice her. Why?'

'No reason,' said Roscoe, 'but I worry about her. Matteo was capable of killing two men in Chicago. I wonder what else he might be capable of.'

'She seemed okay to me,' said Anna. 'Oscar Miller arrived soon after them.'

'Really?' said Roscoe, surprised that the new chairman of the hotel group was in London for Christmas.

'Yes, Enzo Ginevra came down to the foyer to welcome them all and took Miller and Matteo straight into the gin bar. I'm not sure they've come out since.'

'I don't think the Ginevra family would be my choice of Christmas companions.'

'Mine neither,' said Anna, 'although since I'm working most of tomorrow I'm sure I will have the pleasure of their company at some point.'

'You drew the short straw for Christmas Day?' said Roscoe. 'How long are you working for?'

'Until early evening.'

'I'm having dinner here tomorrow night with Martin and Aunt Jessie. You should join us.'

'Are you sure?'

'Absolutely. Martin and I are in St Barnham most of the day and Aunt Jessie is spending the day with her son Alvin and his wife, so we're getting together in the evening.'

'I would love to come,' said Anna with a smile, then she leant across and kissed Roscoe on the cheek.

CHAPTER 16

LATE IN THE EVENING, Roscoe walked through the hotel while its guests enjoyed the finest possible festive hospitality. He took a seat in Tribeca's London Gin Bar and as he did Oscar Miller hastily crossed the room towards him. Uninvited, he pulled up a chair at Roscoe's table.

'Mr Miller?' said Roscoe to the man who thirty years before had partnered Jackson Harlington in establishing the luxury hotel group.

'You need to draw a line under Chicago,' said Miller.

'I'm sorry, sir?'

'You heard me,' said Miller. Roscoe realised Anna had been right in her supposition that the hotel chairman hadn't left the bar all afternoon. 'There are no more witnesses. There is no case to answer.'

'I'm sorry, sir, but—'

'Tribeca Luxury Hotels has worked with Ginevra Construction for over thirty years. Enzo Ginevra was a partner of ours from the very beginning. He helped us build our very first hotel. This ends now.'

'But Mr Miller, this isn't about Enzo, this is about Matteo. And Matteo is guilty. There is no doubt in my mind.'

'Listen, Roscoe, I don't know how to make this any clearer. Either you leave the Ginevra family alone or you're going to be back on the beat plodding round the streets of London. I don't employ you to upset our most important business partner.'

Miller stood up from the table, stumbled back across the bar and resumed his seat at the right hand of Enzo Ginevra.

Two gin martinis were served to Roscoe's table as Anna entered the bar to join him in a Christmas toast. She was closely followed by Matteo Ginevra.

'I don't know why you're wasting your time with him,' he said, brushing up behind Anna.

Refusing to acknowledge him, Anna took a seat beside Roscoe.

Roscoe was riled. A surge of anger raced through him and he started to rise until he felt Anna press a warning hand against his leg.

He knew she was right.

'Your boss has given you your instructions,' Matteo said in Roscoe's ear as he moved past the table. 'Now stay away.'

'You don't even have to tell me he isn't worth it,' said Roscoe, turning to Anna. 'I left Chicago nearly twenty-four hours ago but Chicago doesn't seem to have left me.'

'Relax,' she replied.

'You're right.' Roscoe raised his glass. 'Here's to the most wonderful, happy and peaceful Christmas ever.'

PART 3

Christmas Day

CHAPTER 17

MARIKA ROSCOE KNEW IT was going to be a long day.

Christmas Day with her parents, her estranged husband, her stepson and her young daughters – all thrown together under one roof. Everyone's expectation was for the most wonderful day – and she was the one who would have to deliver it.

Awake early, she crept downstairs, picked up her jacket and opened the back door of her parents' home. Glancing at the clock on the kitchen wall, she saw the hour hand was approaching seven. The girls would be awake any minute.

She stepped out onto the frost-covered lawn, reaching into her pocket for her lighter as she did. One cigarette wouldn't kill her, she told herself. The girls' presents were under the tree, and Santa Claus had done his work. Jon and Martin would be with them before breakfast and she was looking forward to seeing her stepson, whom she hadn't seen for the last three months. For the past nine years Martin had been like a son to her and whatever the future might hold, she never wanted that to end.

The calming warmth of her cigarette kept away the biting cold as she ran through her plans for the day. Nothing would stop the girls opening their presents as soon as they were awake. Chaos would ensue as boxes were ripped open and new toys discovered. She and Jon had bought presents together for their daughters and she wondered if she was being naive in hoping this would always be the case.

Christmas lunch would be in the early afternoon and she had already done most of the preparation; the rest she would hand over to her mother. Umi would have her own way of doing things and that meant there was really only room for one of them in the kitchen. Marika told herself she could cope with that as she reached into her pocket for a second cigarette.

After all, it was going to be a long day.

Surrounded by silence, she stood in the darkness at the rear of the house, looking up at the clear night sky. Anticipating the excitement her daughters would bring to the day, her contentment was abruptly shattered as the Montgomeries' house alarm once again burst into life. Its penetrating wail cut through her and she felt a growing sympathy for her mother's point of view. Did this alarm go off every night?

But as quickly as it had started the alarm was silenced.

Marika took one last draw from her cigarette, then dropped it to the ground and crushed it under her foot. About to step back inside the house, she heard a woman's scream coming from next door.

The scream was repeated over and over, and Marika quickly made her way through into Dame Annabel's garden towards the back of the house. For a second she paused when she saw that the rear door, boarded up since the attack the night before, had been forced open. Was an intruder still inside?

In the darkness, Marika pushed through the door to find herself standing in the now silent kitchen.

She called out. Was anyone there?

Warily she walked through the kitchen and into the hallway. She called again, before another terrifying cry came from behind her on the stairs.

Marika felt along the wall for a light switch and as she lit up the hallway she discovered Emily Lee staggering down the stairs. Convulsed with tears and unable to catch her breath, all she could do was call desperately for help.

At first Marika thought Emily had been assaulted, such was the crippling physical pain she appeared to be in. Marika took hold of her, telling her to take a deep breath.

'Brayden has gone!' Emily hollered. 'My little boy has been taken!'

CHAPTER 18

'GONE FROM HIS ROOM?' asked Marika, seeing the horror consuming Emily.

'The alarm went off – I got straight out of bed, I ran into Brayden's room, switched on the light but he wasn't there,' cried Emily, still gasping for breath as she spoke.

'Emily, what's going on?' called Dame Annabel from the top of the stairs as she emerged from her bedroom.

Emily turned and looked despairingly up the stairs at her mother. 'It's Brayden. I can't find him. I went into his room when the alarm went off but he's gone.'

Dame Annabel quickly made her way down the three steps to her daughter.

'Look at me and calm down,' she said. 'Brayden's not in his bed? Is that what you are saying?'

Emily nodded.

'He's a two-year-old boy in a strange house,' said Annabel. 'He could easily have climbed out of bed and wandered downstairs. It could have been him that set the alarm off. Or maybe he heard the alarm and was scared. I thought it was one of you moving about so I hit the reset button. He's probably hidden somewhere in the house. Let's begin a search and we'll soon have him found.'

'I don't think Brayden has wandered off,' said Marika.

'I'm sorry?' said Annabel, looking at Marika for the first time.

'I came in through the back of the house. The door has been forced open. As far as I can see, somebody's been in.'

'No!' screamed Emily, scrambling back up the stairs towards her son's room. 'Brayden!' The other two women followed her up.

'First thing we need to do is search the house,' said Dame Annabel, attempting to remain calm.

'I really think you need to see downstairs,' said Marika. 'Somebody's been in and we have to assume they've taken Brayden.'

'Wyatt!' called Dame Annabel. He appeared at his bedroom door, his beer gut hanging over his shorts.

'What the hell?' said Wyatt, rubbing his eyes. 'Enough with the screaming.'

'Your son is missing,' said Dame Annabel to her son-in-law.

'What?' He appeared only semi-conscious.

'He's gone from his bed,' said Marika.

'What are you talking about?'

'I suggest you speak to your wife if you don't believe me.'

'Emily!' shouted Wyatt. Marika smelt the stale stench of alcohol as he pushed past her towards his son's bedroom. 'Where is he?' he yelled. 'Don't mess me about. Tell me what you've done with him.'

Marika followed Wyatt into Brayden's room and saw Emily physically shake as she cowered at the side of her son's empty bed.

'You've taken him, I know you have!' he yelled at his wife. 'You wanted to get him away from me! You never wanted me here. We should be back home in Chicago.' He loomed over her. 'Where is he?'

Ready to defend Emily, Marika stepped forward. 'You need to calm down, Wyatt,' she said, seeing his surprise at her challenging him. 'This won't help find Brayden. There's been a break-in downstairs. Somebody has been in the house.'

CHAPTER 19

SANTA CLAUS SAT RESPLENDENT in his red-and-gold sleigh, beneath the magnificent Christmas tree in the marbled foyer of London's Tribeca Luxury Hotel. Excitement buzzed through the hotel as Tribeca brought its very own special magic to the day. Watching Saint Nick arrive with gifts for every guest and member of staff, Anna Conquest remembered why she loved Christmas Day at the hotel chain.

The first visitors of the day to be greeted by Santa Claus were Harper Ginevra and her big sister, Cal. Anna watched them walk hand in hand across the foyer before Cal, her blonde hair strikingly swept back, crouched beside her sister as they were wished a happy Christmas. Both girls collected parcels that they gratefully accepted before walking away to find themselves a quiet corner of the foyer, where they sat alone.

Thinking of the conversation she had had with Jon on Christmas Eve, Anna couldn't help but walk across and speak to the two girls. 'Merry Christmas,' she said to them.

Harper, her hair tied back in pigtails and already wearing her Christmas party dress, curled into her sister.

'Hi,' Cal said. 'We're okay sitting here?'

'Absolutely,' said Anna. 'I only wanted to come over to see what Santa Claus had brought you.'

Harper lifted her head and showed Anna a beautiful hand-stitched white teddy bear, personalised with her name.

'Wow,' said Anna, crouching down to talk to Harper. 'He's a very smart bear, isn't he?'

Harper nodded and smiled.

'What are you going to call him?'

'Frosty,' said Harper.

'That's a great name,' said Anna. 'And I love your red dress. It's very beautiful.'

'Thank you,' said Harper quietly.

'And the ribbons in your hair match your dress. Did your mummy help you with those?'

'No, Cal did them,' said Harper.

'I think they look wonderful,' said Anna to both girls.

'Shall we see what he brought me?' said Cal to her sister, starting to open her parcel. 'What do you think it might be?'

'Jewels,' said Harper.

'I don't think it'll be jewels,' said Cal, 'but it is something in a nice box.'

'A watch!' said Harper as Cal opened an Orla Kiely gift box. 'I can tell the time,' she added proudly, quickly turning her attention back to Anna.

'Can you?' said Anna. 'You are a very clever girl. How old are you?'

'I'm four but I will be five in March.'

'Can you remember what date in March?'

'March ninth,' confirmed Harper. 'And then I'll get more presents.'

'Hopefully,' added Cal, smiling at her.

'And have you got lots of presents today?' asked Anna.

'Lots,' said Harper, her eyes wide open.

'But we're not opening them until after lunch, are we?' said Cal.

Harper shook her head.

'I hope you get everything you wished for,' said Anna. 'Have a wonderful day.'

She stood up and was about to walk away when Cal called her back. 'Do you work with Jon Roscoe?' she asked.

'Yes, I do,' said Anna.

'And he's a good guy?'

'Why do you ask?' Anna was intrigued by Cal's interest.

'I met him in Chicago and he seemed like a pretty nice guy.'

'He is,' said Anna. 'He's one of the best.'

'Is he around today?'

'He'll be in later,' she replied. 'Is there anything I can help you with?'

'No, not right now,' said Cal, getting to her feet and reaching down to pick up her sister. 'But I have a feeling I might need him later.'

CHAPTER 20

WYATT LEE RAN OUT the front of Dame Annabel's house into the middle of the village. Yelling his son's name, he began to run erratically around St Barnham.

'Why won't people leave me alone?' said Dame Annabel as she supported her frail daughter out the front of the house. 'They can say what they like about me online, but don't take it out on my family!' she cried out into the darkness. 'Some religious freak has been offended by one of my books and now they're taking their revenge. That's what this is all about, I'm sure of it. Don't you think so, Marika?'

'It could be,' replied Marika, not ready to jump to any conclusions.

'I'm certain it is,' continued Dame Annabel. 'What else could it possibly be? I should have done more to protect us. I've turned us all into targets.'

Marika said nothing as Wyatt ran towards the duck pond and then tore around its frozen edge, calling for his son. 'Brayden!' he cried at the top of his voice. 'Brayden!'

'He's gone, hasn't he?' said Emily, standing at Marika's side.

'The police will be here any minute and they'll get a proper search started,' said Marika. She quickly messaged her husband. Then, seeing that Emily was in shock, she looked for Dame Annabel to take her daughter back inside.

She was nowhere to be seen.

Putting her arm around Emily, Marika helped her back towards the house. Her eye was caught by a light in the house opposite. Wyatt's cries were certain to wake the village but as Marika turned she saw a man standing motionless at the window of that house. As she walked Emily back inside he remained still, silhouetted at the window.

Julian Templeton was eager to observe the commotion breaking out in the village. He dimmed the lights in his living room in the hope of not being seen but as Wyatt ran around the pond, the American looked directly at him.

Julian shivered and quickly stepped away from his window, out of sight.

But it was too late.

'What are you looking at?' screamed Wyatt. 'I can still see you,' he shouted as Julian edged further behind his blind. 'You're never away from that window. What did you see?'

Wyatt started to move towards Julian's house, walking at first and then breaking into a run. 'Tell me what you saw!'

Dame Annabel appeared in the doorway of her house and gave her arm to her daughter. 'Come inside, darling,' she said. Then she and Marika turned as, without warning, Wyatt charged at the front door of Julian's small house. Running forward, he slammed into it with his shoulder. The door shuddered but stood firm. Wyatt retreated, pacing back up the path before turning and charging again.

Once more the door stood firm.

'Open the door!' he yelled, hammering his fists against the door. 'Get out here and tell me what you saw!'

Inside the house, Julian Templeton held his breath. He prayed the door would hold.

Wyatt walked out of the garden to the edge of the pond. 'You can hide away as much as you like,' he yelled up at the window, 'but I'm coming to get you!'

Marika ran across the road as he grabbed a rock from beside the pond and made his way back into the man's garden.

'No!' she shouted as he walked back towards the house. 'This won't help find Brayden.'

But Wyatt Lee never broke his stride. He ran at the house. This time, though, he hurled a rock through the living-room window. The glass smashed, shards flying into the house.

Julian Templeton froze.

'You know something!' roared Wyatt. 'I've seen you at that window, hour after hour. Whatever you saw, I'm going to find out!'

Julian Templeton felt a single bead of sweat run down his spine. Closing his eyes, he prayed that Wyatt never would.

CHAPTER 21

THE EARLY-MORNING WINTER DARKNESS still hung over the village as Roscoe drove into St Barnham. With his son Martin by his side he was looking forward to Christmas Day with his wife and children. Pulling up outside the home of Marika's parents, he picked up his phone and read the message she had just sent him.

Today wasn't going to be the day he had imagined.

Stepping from his car, he looked across the road and saw Marika standing by the gate of the small house that neighboured the village pond. Beyond her, he could see the damage done to the window of the house. He walked across to her and as he did Wyatt Lee came running from the garden.

Oblivious to his arrival, Wyatt crashed into Roscoe as he charged out into the village, still calling the name of his son.

'Enough,' said Roscoe, taking hold of him. 'You need to calm down.'

'My son has been taken!' screamed Wyatt.

'I know,' replied Roscoe with an authoritative calm. 'And we will all need to work with the police to find him. Tell me what's happened.'

'He knows something, I know he does!' shouted Wyatt. He flailed his arms and struggled to free himself.

Roscoe tightened his grip, locking his hands on Wyatt's shoulders and looking directly at him. 'I said enough. Who knows something?'

'That freak,' said Wyatt. 'Always standing at his window, looking out day and night. He must have seen something. Somebody must have seen something.'

Roscoe eased his grip. 'The police will talk to him; they'll speak to everyone in the village.' Hearing the sound of police sirens approaching, he put his arm around Wyatt and turned him back towards Dame Annabel's home. 'Let's go in the house. It will be easier for you to talk to the police inside.' Turning to Marika, he asked if a proper search of the village had begun.

'Nothing yet,' said Marika.

'We can help with that,' he replied. 'Brayden could have just wandered outside.'

'I don't think so,' said Marika. 'Somebody's broken through the boarding at the back of the house – and it wasn't a two-year-old boy.'

Walking towards the front of the Montgomerie house, Roscoe looked at Marika with genuine concern. 'Missing children are nearly always found somewhere near their home,' he said. 'Let's hope that's the case here.'

Suddenly Dame Annabel appeared at the door of her home. 'Marika, come quickly!' she called. 'Emily's not breathing!'

CHAPTER 22

WITH TWO YOUNG DAUGHTERS spellbound by the excitement of Santa Claus and the magic he delivers on Christmas Day, Marika knew she had to continue her family celebrations even if only in a perfunctory way after the horrors of the morning.

Sitting at her parents' dining table as Martin cleared the dessert plates from the family's Christmas lunch, she felt she had an enormous amount to be grateful for. Umi loved to tell her what a fine young man Martin had become and Marika had no reason to disagree. The great maturity he showed as a fifteen-year-old boy was in huge part due to his father, and with them all sitting around the dining table Marika had realised how much she missed having all of her family together.

She couldn't help thinking of the devastation the Montgomeries were suffering. And while her own daughters sat in the corner of the dining room sharing the delights of Barbie's Malibu beach house, she found it impossible to imagine the agony being suffered by Emily, Wyatt and Annabel. A police car was parked outside their house and interviews continued, but there was still no trace of their missing son.

Emily had fallen into extreme shock and once Marika had stabilised her, she had been taken to the Chelsea and Westminster Hospital, where she remained sedated and under observation.

'Dad, what will happen next in the search for Brayden?' asked Martin as he collected the plates from around the table.

'The police will keep going with house-to-house; it's possible somebody did see something during the night. Forensics will work inside the house and should be able to find traces left by the abductors, but they'll need more than that to bring him home.'

'Poor Annabel,' said Umi. 'We are so lucky to have such a wonderful neighbour. She doesn't deserve this.'

Marika glanced at Roscoe.

'I was thinking I might drop round later this afternoon, just to see how she's coping,' continued Umi.

'It might be a little bit soon, don't you think, Mama?' said Marika. 'Maybe you should wait until we've had some more news.'

'Perhaps you're right,' said Umi. 'I can't begin to think how guilty she must be feeling. After all, it's her writings that have created this whole horrible situation.'

'Do you think it's some kind of religious group?' asked Marika, looking back at Roscoe.

'It's possible,' he replied. 'But there has been no claim of responsibility or demands made. So if it is a religious group, what do they want?'

'I keep thinking about the night before,' said Marika. 'I was stood at my window and I saw the man run from in front of the house out into the village. He must have been the one who sprayed the car. But it was over two hours later when the alarm went off.'

'I'm surprised you didn't go outside chasing after him,' said Umi. 'Just think what might have happened to you. You should leave all that chasing to Jon.'

'Mama, I didn't go chasing after anybody.'

'Didn't go chasing? First they threw a brick through the back door, the alarm was ringing and there you were outside in your nightclothes. And then the boy goes missing and you were first into the house. You behave like a policewoman, not a doctor. I worry about you up in Edinburgh. You'd be so much safer back here in London, wouldn't she, Jon?'

Roscoe smiled at his mother-in-law. 'I'm sure Marika can look after herself,' he said, 'although it would be nice to have everyone back home in London.'

'I can only wish,' said Umi. 'I would sleep so much better at night if I knew that was the case.'

'What I don't understand is,' said Marika's father, leaning back in his chair at the head of the table, 'if they attacked the house the previous night, why didn't they take the boy then?'

'Maybe the alarm scared them off,' said Martin.

'And why spray the car and then come back later to smash the door?' asked Marika.

'Maybe it wasn't them who came back,' said Roscoe.

'Not *two* sets of crazy people!' said Umi. 'Surely not, Jon, please God.'

'Talk me through what happened this morning,' Roscoe said to his wife.

'I was outside, getting some air.'

'Smoking,' said Umi. 'Don't think I don't know. You've started that again since living in Edinburgh.'

'I was outside getting some air,' repeated Marika. 'It was around seven, just before, I think, and the alarm went off for no more than five seconds.'

'And that's when Dame Annabel says she hit the reset button?' asked Roscoe.

'Yes. And then less than a minute later I heard screams coming from Emily.'

'She's discovered that her poor son was missing,' said Umi to Roscoe, in case he wasn't following.

Roscoe nodded in Marika's direction. 'You go straight to the house, the boarded-up door has been forced open, you go inside and Emily comes down the stairs?'

'Yes,' said Marika.

'So whoever broke in and took Brayden had to force the door, race upstairs, grab him, run back down and be clear of the garden in less than ninety seconds. Otherwise you would have seen them?'

'Yes,' she agreed.

'Well, unless our kidnapper was Usain Bolt,' said Roscoe, 'that boy was already gone.'

CHAPTER 23

ROSCOE LIFTED HIS ARM and stretched his shoulder as he walked with his beloved Aunt Jessie across the lawns of London's Tribeca Luxury Hotel.

'Beautiful,' she said to her adopted son as she absorbed the spectacle of the illuminated gardens: every tree decorated with different-coloured lights to create a night-time spectacular.

An afternoon spent assembling his daughters' new slide followed by chasing them around their grandparents' garden had left him looking forward to a quiet late-evening supper at the hotel.

As they walked inside and through the decked hallways, Jessie turned to him. 'Now, tell me, what have you done to that shoulder of yours? You haven't stopped stretching it since you collected me from Alvin's.'

'A bit of a tear – nothing to worry about,' said Roscoe, unconsciously stretching it out again.

'Doesn't look like nothing to me.' Aunt Jessie linked her arm through his. 'Promise me you will have it looked at.'

'I promise,' said Roscoe, pulling her close to him.

Turning into the hallway outside the restaurant, the last person he wanted to see was Matteo Ginevra.

'How sweet,' said Matteo as he stumbled down the hall towards Roscoe and Aunt Jessie. 'Taking the old folk out at Christmas.' Lurching forward, he tried to slap Roscoe on the back.

'You're drunk,' said Roscoe tersely.

'It's Christmas!' replied Matteo. 'A time for celebrating.'

'You've got nothing to celebrate. You're a fool if you think I've gone away.'

'You've got me all wrong, Jon,' said Matteo, grinning broadly. 'And anyway, it's not me who's celebrating, it was good old Jerry Davis.'

'What are you talking about?' said Roscoe.

'Jerry Davis. You remember him, always such a straight-up guy? Gave his evidence to the court, headed down to his new home in Florida to celebrate.'

'And?'

'And he's had a tragic accident. He had a new life, and a beautiful new home on the fourteenth floor of a luxury block. But he celebrated a little too much. The police found him earlier today. You don't need me to tell you a fall from such a height would be impossible to survive. And on Christmas Day. Just tragic.'

'You bastard,' said Roscoe. He pushed Matteo away from him.

'Have a happy Christmas,' said Matteo, falling forwards again.

Roscoe snapped. He slammed Ginevra against the wall, holding him by the throat, crushing his windpipe. Unable to breathe, Matteo's face rapidly turned puce.

It was the moment Roscoe had waited for. Revenge.

He increased the pressure and Matteo collapsed to his knees.

Anger boiling inside him, he forced Matteo to the ground. His fingers tightened around his throat until Ginevra had no breath left to take.

CHAPTER 24

'JON, NO!' SCREAMED AUNT Jessie.

Snapped from his stupor, Roscoe released his grip and tossed Matteo aside.

'Stay away from me,' he said, standing over the Italian. 'Next time one of the old folk might not be around to save you.'

Stepping around Matteo, he took hold of Aunt Jessie's arm and led her into the restaurant. 'I've a table reserved for four,' he told a waiter.

'Please follow me, sir – your other guests have already arrived,' the waiter replied, leading them to where Anna and Martin were already seated.

'I'm sorry,' Roscoe said to Aunt Jessie as they crossed the room.

'I'm sure he deserved it,' she replied, then stopped and took Roscoe's hand. 'My only worry is, Jon, one day I won't be there to stop you.'

*

Coffee was being served at the end of Roscoe's meal when Oscar Miller entered the restaurant. Approaching his table, Miller simply said to his security chief, 'I told you this had to stop.'

'Matteo been telling tales?' said Roscoe, getting to his feet to face Miller but wondering if this time he had gone too far.

'The Ginevra family are irreplaceable associates of Tribeca Luxury Hotels. Our businesses work hand in hand and our success is entwined with theirs. I will not have my global head of security threatening that relationship in any way. Do you understand me?'

'Jerry Davis is dead, sir.'

Miller looked quizzically at Roscoe. 'What are you talking about?'

'Jerry Davis, the witness from Chicago.'

'Roscoe, I told you to leave Chicago alone. I couldn't care less about Jerry Davis, Sammy Davis or Geena Davis. I want you to listen to me. One more incident like this and your time with Tribeca is over.'

Roscoe seethed with fury but remained silent.

'I'm glad you understand,' said Miller. 'To draw a line under this, I want you to go upstairs, apologise to Enzo and tell him you'll leave him, his son and his family alone.'

Staring at Miller, Roscoe swallowed hard. 'Matteo Ginevra was responsible for the death of two construction workers and I now believe he is responsible for the death of Jerry Davis.'

'The twenty-eighth floor,' said Miller. 'Now.'

Roscoe stood with Aunt Jessie beside the magnificent Christmas tree that extended up through the marbled lobby of the Tribeca Luxury Hotel. Holding her close, he wished her goodnight. The woman who had raised him since he was only four years old remained a force for good in his life. He was indebted to her in a way it was impossible for him to ever repay.

As she and Martin climbed into a black cab, Roscoe stood at the entrance to the hotel and watched them disappear down the driveway. As soon as they were gone, he walked across the foyer and hit the call button for the express elevator.

Racing up through the building, he tried to convince himself he had to move on. Scum like Matteo Ginevra weren't worth it. And he wasn't worth the career Roscoe had built at Tribeca. He loved working for the hotel group and all of the challenges it brought him. He wasn't about to let that go.

He had to step back from the brink.

Reaching the twenty-eighth floor, he walked quickly down the hallway and pushed the bell outside Enzo Ginevra's suite.

There was no reply. He pressed again and was about to leave when he heard footsteps approach from within.

Still the door didn't open, so Roscoe knocked gently. He heard the lock being turned and the door slowly opened.

Standing in front of him was Cal Ginevra, her hands and arms smothered with blood.

PART 4

26 December

CHAPTER 25

ROSCOE LOOKED AT CAL Ginevra standing in the doorway of her father's suite. She held her palms open in front of her; her hands and arms were wet with blood.

'Cal?' he said softly, realising she was rigid with shock. 'Cal, you need to step inside and let me in.'

She took one step back from the door and collapsed against the wall. As she dropped to the floor, Roscoe leant forward to catch her. Feeling her bloodied hands slide down his back, she fell lifelessly to the ground.

'Tell me what's happened,' he said. 'Has somebody tried to hurt you?'

Mute, Cal curled into the wall, wrapping herself up tightly. Holding her head in her hands, she smeared the red blood through her white-blonde hair.

Crouching beside her, Roscoe tried to see her face. She turned away.

'Cal, who else is here?' he asked. 'Who else is in the suite?'

She pulled her body tighter into itself.

Roscoe got to his feet and stared into the living room. A single brass banker's lamp lit the room. In the dim glow, he could see blood traced across the oak floor.

Hesitantly, he moved forward through the living room and towards the main bedroom. The door was closed but Roscoe could follow the trail of blood coming from the room.

Slowly he edged the door open.

Inside he could hear the steady drip of blood onto the polished floor. Stepping into the room, he saw the glint of a shining silver blade protruding from the chest of a body lying prone across the bed.

Roscoe inched forward.

He stopped at the side of the bed. The victim's eyes stared up at him, still fixed in terror.

Lying on the king-sized bed, the white Egyptian cotton sheets turned red with blood, was Enzo Ginevra.

CHAPTER 26

ROSCOE LOOKED DOWN ON the ravaged body. It was clear to him a frenzied and ruthless attack had just taken place and that Enzo Ginevra had been repeatedly stabbed in his chest and neck with the silver Tribeca Luxury Hotels carving knife that now jutted from his heart.

Still standing beside the bed, he heard sobs coming from the living room. He walked out of the bedroom and back to the entrance to the suite, where Enzo's daughter Cal remained crouched against the wall.

For a moment he stood in silence, watching Cal rock herself back and forth. What had taken place in Enzo's bedroom was an attack the savagery of which Roscoe had rarely seen. It was as if a fury had been released from within the killer, held deep for many years. Cal was a girl of no more than eighteen. What could have driven her to such an act?

'Tell me what happened,' he repeated.

She continued to rock herself, backwards and forwards.

Roscoe knelt down, placing a hand upon her shoulder. He felt her movement stop and she rested herself back against the wall.

'Is anyone else hurt?'

She slowly shook her head.

'Kellie and Harper?'

Again she shook her head.

'Where are they?' asked Roscoe.

She looked down at her hands, still wet with blood, and ran her fingers across her palms.

'Cal, I need to know where they are.'

'Asleep,' said Cal. 'In my suite. I knew this was my chance.'

'You did this?' said Roscoe, already knowing the answer to his question.

'I was waiting for him.'

'Why?'

Cal shook her head.

Roscoe got to his feet. 'Is there anything you want to tell me before I call the police?'

She started to rock once more.

Roscoe dropped again to his knees. 'Look at me,' he said urgently. 'Why have you done this?'

Cal lifted her head. A single tear ran down her blood-stained face.

'Tell me why you did this, Cal. Why?' Roscoe repeated, his voice rising in frustration.

She looked directly at Roscoe. 'Harper is not my sister,' she whispered. 'She's my daughter.'

CHAPTER 27

A PHYSICAL BLOW COULD not have rocked Roscoe with any greater force.

'Harper's your daughter?'

Cal stared back at the floor and nodded.

'I was thirteen,' she began. 'We lived in an old Italian house with marble floors and heavy wooden doors. Even now when I lie awake at night I can hear the creak of the handle as the door was cracked open and he let himself into my room.

'I think I was seven or eight when it first started. My mother was ill, hardly ever left her room. We often had different people visit the house, all kinds of people coming and going. I never really understood how sick my mother was, I just wanted her to be well again.

'Each time he came I wished so hard she would come and save me. Months and then years went by. I saw my mother less and less. All she could do was lie in her bed. She was so very weak.

'More and more he came to my room. Each time I closed my eyes and pretended I was asleep. He didn't care.

'And then one day . . . one day I knew, there was a baby coming.'

Roscoe could only imagine the agony Cal had carried with her for so many years. His urge was to hold her, to take her into his arms and tell her he would make everything all right. But he knew he couldn't. He knew nothing would ever be all right for her again.

She looked up at him, her face streaked with blood and tears. 'My father sent me away. He had another house, hidden away in the hills. I promised him I'd be good but he still sent me away. My mother was dead and he was marrying Kellie. He told her I'd been stupid with a boy from school. My baby was born and two days later my father took her away from me. I cried and cried for my little girl. I wanted her so badly.

'He sent me away to school in America. I never saw Harper again. Until now. I told him I couldn't live without her any longer. He told me to forget about her, that she would never be mine. I couldn't do that. I had to have her, to protect her from the very same thing that happened to me.'

Cal paused.

'I was ready for him.'

CHAPTER 28

IN THE DARKNESS OF the early hours of the morning, Roscoe stood in the foyer of the Tribeca Luxury Hotel. With Anna at his side, he watched as first Cal was led away by the Metropolitan Police and then the body of Enzo Ginevra was carried from the hotel.

'You think she planned it?' asked Anna.

'She definitely planned it,' replied Roscoe. 'She put Harper to sleep in her own bed, sent Kellie in to sleep with her and then let herself into Enzo's suite. Half drunk, he had drifted off to sleep and she was waiting for him.' He shivered. 'Years of rage poured out of her. I've never seen an attack so frenetic.'

'What will happen now?'

'I'm sure she'll be charged. My old boss, Fran Walker, is heading up the case, but whatever happens, this was a most violent and premeditated attack,' he sighed. 'And I should have seen it coming.'

Anna put her hand on his arm. 'Nobody could have seen this coming.'

'But she was desperate for help. If I'd pushed her harder, made her tell me what was going on in her head, understood her desperation to protect her daughter, I could have prevented this. But I didn't. I was distracted, so determined to get Matteo that I didn't see what was right in front of me.' He stretched his shoulder and remembered the sight of Cal running across the snow-covered road only three days before. 'I knew there was evil in that family.'

Oscar Miller walked into the foyer.

'Please, Jon, don't do anything stupid,' said Anna.

'I won't,' he said, turning towards his boss. 'Are you happy now, Mr Miller?'

Oscar Miller stopped and faced Roscoe. He looked exhausted, overrun by stress and fear. 'What did you say?' he said.

'I told you the Ginevra family was evil. What do you think drove Cal to do what she did?'

'This is a tragedy but it changes nothing,' said Miller. 'That girl was mentally unwell. Enzo did everything he possibly could for her. She's been held in a secure school for the past four years and he was desperate for her to be part of the family again. The doctors advised against it but he was determined to have all his family together this Christmas. The tragedy is he paid with his life.'

Roscoe took a step back. Could he have been so wrong about Cal? Is that why she never truly confided in him?

'Mr Miller,' he said with a slight hesitation, 'the Cal I met wasn't disturbed or from a special school. She was a girl crying out for help.'

'I imagine you hardly spoke more than a few words to her,' said Miller, putting his hand on Roscoe's arm. 'It happens to us all, Jon. She's beautiful and you were drawn in by her, but that doesn't stop her being a fantasist.'

Roscoe took a deep breath. He wanted to shout at Miller that he had got it all wrong. But then he thought of the way she had acted towards him. And how he had convinced himself she needed saving.

And how he was the one to save her.

'Enzo made sure she had the very best treatment money could buy,' continued Miller. 'No one could have foreseen the tragedy that followed.'

'What about her child?' asked Roscoe, just as Matteo Ginevra walked into the foyer.

But Oscar Miller was already walking away from him. For a second Roscoe saw him hesitate, and then he embraced Matteo.

Roscoe watched as the two men headed out the front of the hotel, Miller's arm around Matteo's shoulder.

Cal had been desperate for his help, he told himself. She had needed him and he'd failed her.

So why would Oscar Miller lie to him?

CHAPTER 29

SITTING IN HOLIDAY TRAFFIC as he drove west across London, Roscoe rubbed his eyes. Five years earlier, when serving as an inspector in London's Metropolitan Police, three hours' sleep would have comfortably carried him through the next day. Now, thinking of his judgement of the Ginevra family, he felt anxious and exhausted. He would be thirty-seven early in the new year. Perhaps age was starting to catch up with him.

Greeted by the picturesque scene in the village of St Barnham, its Christmas tree lights still shining, its winding pathways turned white by the frost, he let his mind drift and thought of the secrets the village kept hidden beneath its charming facade.

At the gate to the front garden of his in-laws' home, Roscoe stopped for a moment. Lauren and Aimee were joyously chasing each other around their new slide, climbing up it, sweeping down, and then doing it all over again. Marika sat on the edge of a wooden bench beneath a giant frost-covered fir tree, a steaming-hot cup of coffee clasped between her hands. Laughter filled the air and Roscoe cherished the moment which was in such contrast to the horrors he had witnessed in the hours before. Seeing his daughters lifted his spirits but also reminded him how much he missed them.

'Daddy!' cried Lauren, standing on top of the slide. 'Watch me!'

Stepping into the garden, Roscoe smiled as his daughter threw herself head first down the slide.

'Be careful!' called Marika. Roscoe came and sat beside her on the bench. 'She definitely takes more after you.'

'And Aimee takes after you?' said Roscoe as they watched her follow her sister straight down.

'They are as crazy as each other,' said Marika.

'I do miss you all.'

'And they miss you.'

'And you?' said Roscoe after a pause.

'Let's not do this now, Jon.' Marika got to her feet.

'Do what?' said Roscoe. 'I love you and I want you to come home.'

He took her hand but as he did a police car stopped out on the roadside and Dame Annabel climbed out of the back. Roscoe and Marika crossed the garden to speak to her.

'How is Emily?' asked Marika.

'She's heavily sedated,' said Dame Annabel, standing by her neighbours' gate. 'I've tried to talk to her but in the state she's in it's impossible to get any sense. If I could just get through to her, I'm sure it would make a difference.'

'I'm sure she'll be fine,' said Marika, 'but a shock like this hits people in different ways.'

'I thought I would be able to get through to her.'

'Perhaps by tomorrow,' said Marika.

'Yes, perhaps,' said Dame Annabel, anxiously looking towards her own house. 'Any news here?'

'Not that we're aware of,' said Roscoe. 'I'm sure the police are doing everything possible.'

'I'm sure they are,' said Dame Annabel, 'but all I can do is think of my grandson and the desperate danger he's in.'

The front door of the small house opposite the Montgomerie home was suddenly thrown open and its owner, Julian Templeton, scurried across the road towards them. With only slippers on his feet, wearing a chunky, knitted sweater, loose-fitting trousers and thick-framed black glasses, he cut an eccentric figure.

'I need to speak with you now,' he said to Dame Annabel, ignoring Roscoe and his wife. 'I need to speak with you urgently.'

'Julian,' said Dame Annabel, a sharp edge in her voice. 'I'm sure you're very aware that my family have a huge amount to deal with right now. Perhaps we might talk a little later, or tomorrow, when things have become a little clearer.'

'Clearer, you say?' said Templeton in a clipped tone. 'That is no use to me. I need you now.'

'And I need to go inside and understand where the police have got to in the search for my grandson. I will try to speak with you later.'

Templeton's face reddened and he pursed his lips. 'But I—'

'No, Julian,' said Dame Annabel. 'Go back to your house, sit in your window and take pleasure in watching the horrors the rest of us are having to endure.'

Dismissed, Julian Templeton walked back inside his house and silently closed the door behind him. Anger rose within him.

His meticulous preparations had not been mirrored by others. He had done everything that had been asked of him and had been unquestioning in his loyalty.

Now he was the one in danger.

He could still see the fury in Wyatt Lee's eyes when he had approached his door. He had never agreed to be placed in a position of peril.

And now to be dismissed like a scolded child. He wouldn't be treated in that way.

Someone needed to be taught a lesson.

CHAPTER 30

AS DAME ANNABEL WENT into her home, Roscoe watched Julian Templeton walk around the inside of his home and close each of the window blinds. He imagined him sitting alone in the darkness.

'He seems like an unusual character,' he said to Marika. Squeals of delight continued to come from his daughters as they chased each other around the garden.

'Julian?' said Marika. 'I think he's harmless. He's lived in that house as long as I can remember. I guess I'd call him the village eccentric. And he'd do anything for Dame Annabel. I think he's been secretly in love with her for years.'

'I know that feeling,' said Roscoe.

'Who have you been secretly in love with?'

'Maybe not secretly,' said Roscoe. They sat once again on the bench, watching their daughters.

'Jon,' said Marika, turning to her husband, 'you know part of me will—'

Roscoe interrupted her. 'All I want is for us all to be back together in our home, living as a family. Please, Marika.'

'Don't, Jon,' said Marika, getting to her feet and turning away. 'Our lives are so different. You live in a world with some of the wealthiest and most powerful people and it means—'

'I try to make time for you and the children.'

'I know, but you called me at two in the morning to tell me a man had been murdered.' She turned back to him. 'How do you think that makes me feel?'

'I didn't want you hearing it on the news,' said Roscoe. 'It's my job, Marika.' He went to his wife and put his arm around her.

She stepped away.

'But it's a job that leaves very little time for your family,' she said.

'I'm always there for the girls.'

'I know you are, but when I say no time for your family, I mean no time for me. I don't fit into your life any more.'

She paused and Roscoe held his breath. Somehow he knew what she was going to say.

'You've met someone else?' he said.

'It's early days, Jon,' she said. 'I should have already told you but I didn't want to turn it into something it isn't. And it might not go anywhere, but he's kind and the girls like him and most importantly he's there, Jon, and you're not.'

Standing in the garden of Marika's parents' house on a cold winter's morning, Roscoe felt the wife and family he treasured so deeply slipping away from him. The sadness threatened to overwhelm him.

'Are you saying this is it for us?' he asked, always having believed he and Marika would one day get back together.

'I don't know, but my life is in Scotland now,' Marika said softly. 'The girls are at a great school. I enjoy my work and I've made new friends. I'm so sorry.'

'But if we were all here together in London, you'd feel differently, I know you would,' he pleaded. 'I love you, Marika, and I want us to be together. I won't let you go.'

Marika gently kissed him on the cheek. 'Part of me will always love you, but our lives have drifted apart in so many ways. I'm not sure anything will ever bring us back together.'

CHAPTER 31

AN AFTERNOON SPENT PLAYING with his daughters had done little to dispel the anguish racing around Roscoe's mind. As he drove into the underground parking lot at the London Tribeca Luxury Hotel, he reflected on how he had never needed Marika more at a time when she seemed to be moving further away.

Families were disintegrating all around him. He recalled the anger surfacing in Wyatt Lee as he'd desperately searched for his son; the pain suffered by Cal Ginevra at the hands of her own family. He was determined to keep his own family together.

Stepping out of his car, Roscoe clicked his key fob and headed towards the hotel. As he did so, a man walked out of the exit and in the half-light, Roscoe took a moment to realise he was heading directly for him. Walking erratically and seeming to ignore all around him, the man focused in on Roscoe.

Twenty feet away, the man stopped.

Roscoe looked as Oscar Miller stood motionless, fixed rigidly to the spot.

'Mr Miller?' said Roscoe, looking at him through the gloom.

His hands pressed firmly in his coat pockets, Miller didn't move.

Roscoe slowly stepped forward so that he was now standing no more than ten feet away from him.

'You need to understand that Enzo's death changes nothing,' said Miller. 'I want you to stay away from Matteo Ginevra and all his family. They are no concern of yours. Matteo runs the business now and its relationship with Tribeca remains unharmed.'

Roscoe didn't want another argument with Miller, so he walked past him and headed straight into the hotel.

'Don't turn your back on me!' Miller shouted. 'If you don't keep away from the Ginevra family I will bring your time with Tribeca to an end!'

Roscoe kept walking.

'Roscoe!' shouted Miller.

But Roscoe was gone.

The Tribeca London Gin Bar was packed with revellers who Roscoe could see would be celebrating Christmas all the way through to New Year. To help him forget about

Marika and the state of his marriage, he felt like joining them.

When he'd ordered a third round of gin cocktails, he clicked on his phone and hit the number for Chief Inspector Fran Walker.

'Any news?' said Roscoe, knowing Walker never liked to waste time with pleasantries.

'Nothing,' said Walker. 'It's as if the boy was taken from the house and then disappeared into thin air. I'm going to send the team back tomorrow and go harder in the village. Somebody must have seen something.'

'And the attack from the night before? Any religious groups it could be pinned on?'

'I don't see it, Jon. We've checked on all the usual suspects and nothing. And taking a two-year-old boy is one hell of a step up from spraying a bit of paint on a fancy gold car.'

Roscoe smiled. He agreed with Walker that the answer to Brayden's disappearance lay elsewhere.

'As they say, we are pursuing all possible lines of investigation,' she continued.

Roscoe laughed at the line he had used a million times himself. 'Of course you are,' he said. 'And Cal Ginevra?'

'What about her?' said Walker.

'Has she told you anything more about her brother?'

For a moment Walker was silent.

'Jon, I know you've got history with the brother, but what I'm dealing with is a girl who has brutally murdered her father.'

'Yes, but Fran, the brother is the key. I know he is. You should talk to him as well.'

'You found her smothered in her father's blood. How can the brother be the key?' said Walker. 'Anyway, right now she's not saying anything. We'll charge her in the morning.'

'But—'

'Leave it, Jon.'

Walker disconnected the call and Roscoe picked up his two gin cocktails and walked back to his table.

'Who was that?' asked Anna as she took her drink from him.

'Fran Walker,' he replied. 'Still nothing on Brayden.'

'Must be so tough for his parents.'

'And she won't speak to Matteo.'

'You can't fight every battle,' said Anna.

'That's what everybody keeps telling me.'

'Sometimes even you have to listen.'

'I'm missing something, I know I am,' he said. 'I keep thinking of Cal in that bedroom. She let Enzo climb into bed, drift off to sleep and by the time he realised what was happening it was impossible for him to defend himself. I'll never forget the intensity of the attack.' Roscoe rubbed his temples as he thought of the blood-soaked bed.

'I guess for her it was a release,' said Anna. 'She did it for herself and for her daughter. I saw them together on Christmas Day. All she wanted was to be with her.'

'And Enzo wouldn't let her.'

'He stole her child away from her,' said Anna.

'So she killed him.'

Anna looked at Roscoe and nodded.

'She was thirteen when she had Harper,' said Roscoe. 'Her mother was dying and he would go to her room.'

'Jon,' said Anna, reaching across the table and taking his hand, 'don't torture yourself.'

'She told me how, when he came to her, she would pretend to be asleep but he didn't care. I thought she meant Enzo. But did she? She hated Enzo for taking her child, but who was she most afraid of? Who did she run from in Chicago?'

Roscoe looked down at their hands entwined together and then up into Anna's eyes.

'Matteo.'

CHAPTER 32

IT WAS ALMOST MIDNIGHT, and Roscoe stood in front of the bathroom mirror in the bedroom he used when he stayed overnight at the hotel. He splashed water on his face and tried to remember how many double gins he had drunk earlier that evening. He decided it wasn't worth the effort.

Through the open bathroom door he could see Anna lying in bed, her long dark hair around her bare shoulders. She was beautiful, but was this how he went about putting his marriage back together? He thought of his last conversation with Marika. Did they still have a marriage worth saving?

'I've been thinking,' he called.

'Leave it until the morning!' she replied.

'You're right,' he said, popping his head out of the bathroom, 'but if Matteo is the father of Cal's little girl, that would explain everything: why was Cal so frightened; why did she run at the airport; why was she so desperate for my help; why didn't she dare say anything? All because of Matteo.'

Anna stepped out of bed and walked into the bathroom. Putting her arms around Roscoe, she told him not to think about Matteo Ginevra, at least for a couple of hours.

'I can't stand the thought of him still being in the hotel,' said Roscoe.

'Then call Fran Walker in the morning.'

'You're right,' he said as a room-service waiter buzzed at the door.

'Food at last!' said Anna. She stepped out of the bathroom, throwing on one of the hotel's sumptuous robes.

Roscoe watched her in the mirror as she bent to look through the peephole. Then, hearing a click, instantly launched himself towards her, knocking her sideways as a single gunshot exploded through the glass.

PART 5

27 December

CHAPTER 33

A WATERY SUN STOLE through the branches of the bare winter trees as Roscoe knelt and carefully placed a small bouquet of flowers on the neatly tended grave in the cold London cemetery. With Martin beside him, he said a silent prayer to his sister, Amanda.

Fourteen years earlier to the day, Roscoe had made the impossible decision to switch off his sister's life support. Now, kneeling in silence, he could remember each painful moment of that heartbreaking day. Amanda had been attacked four days before while walking home from celebrating her nineteenth birthday. Sitting beside Amanda's hospital bed with his Aunt Jessie and her son, Alvin, Roscoe had taken the hardest decision he hoped he would ever have to make. Having spoken with Alvin on the prognosis, he had watched as the doctors disconnected Amanda's life support. Holding his sister's hand, he had said goodbye.

That evening he had returned home from the hospital and held Martin in his arms. A child of only eighteen months, he had appeared so vulnerable, and Roscoe had made him a promise to be the best father to him he could possibly be. Fourteen years later he was still trying to live up to that promise every single day.

Getting to his feet, Roscoe laid his hand across Martin's back.

'We should go,' he said.

They walked in silence down the gravel pathway and back to Roscoe's waiting SUV.

They approached the car and he clicked the fob. 'I'll be one minute,' said Roscoe. While Martin climbed into the car, he pressed his phone and dialled a number he'd already called three times that morning.

'Hello again,' said Anna, picking up her phone. 'You really don't have to keep checking up on me.'

'I just want to be sure you're safe.'

'Jon, there are police all over the hotel. I'm safer here than anywhere else.'

'And you promise me you're okay?'

'Absolutely,' she assured him. 'I'm more worried about you. When we hit the ground and you crashed into your shoulder, I thought it was you who was going to end up in hospital.'

'It aches a little bit, but give it a day or two and it'll be fine.'

'Haven't you said that before?'

Roscoe laughed. 'Hopefully now I can give it a bit of rest. Have the police found anything on the CCTV?'

'Still nothing,' said Anna. 'The cameras were disengaged ten minutes before the shot was fired.'

'Promise me you'll call if you need anything.'

'I promise,' said Anna, before clicking off the phone.

Roscoe walked back over to his car and climbed in alongside Martin.

'How was Anna?' said Martin.

Roscoe looked at him in surprise.

'Please, Dad,' said Martin, 'I'm not stupid.'

'I was just checking in with her,' said Roscoe.

'For the fourth time this morning?'

Roscoe smiled.

'So, when that shot was fired,' said Martin, 'why were you and Anna in the same bedroom?'

Roscoe ran his hand through his hair self-consciously and turned to his son, who was grinning back at his father. 'You're too young to worry about that.'

'I'm not worried, Dad,' said Martin. 'But does this mean you and Marika are going to divorce?'

Driving out of the cemetery, Roscoe wasn't sure he liked where the conversation was headed. After a moment he stuttered through a reply.

'Sometimes adults do things that maybe they might regret or equally might not regret, but still might look at them differently the next day or at another time.'

'Please, Dad,' said Martin, 'I'm not twelve. What you're trying to say is you and Anna was just sex. That's cool.'

Roscoe wasn't sure *what* he was saying, so he decided to end the conversation there.

CHAPTER 34

DRIVING ACROSS LONDON, ROSCOE hit the speed dial on his phone and called Chief Inspector Fran Walker.

'Fran, it's Roscoe.'

'I heard what happened at the hotel. You okay?'

'We're fine,' said Roscoe. 'A little shaken up, but now I need a favour from you.'

'No harm in asking,' replied Walker.

'I need to speak to Cal Ginevra.'

'Can't do it.'

'Hear me out, Chief. She can give us the answers we need, I'm sure of it. Not just about the Ginevras but about the shooting last night as well. And if she's going to talk to anyone, she'll talk to me.'

There was silence on the phone.

'Chief?'

'I'm looking for a notepad to write my resignation on,' said Walker, 'because if the Super ever hears about this . . .'

'That's a yes?'

'I can give you ten minutes with her,' replied Walker, 'but this had better deliver.'

'I'll be there in five.'

'Five?' Walker's voice rose in surprise. 'You knew I was going to say yes.'

'Only because you trust me,' said Roscoe as he disconnected the call.

Exactly five minutes later, Roscoe walked into the police interview room at New Scotland Yard. Cal was sitting alone at the interrogation table. She looked up at him and he could see the desolation that had long since replaced the bright shine of her deep brown eyes.

'Hello again,' he said, taking the seat opposite her. 'I'm here to help, if you'll let me.'

'It's too late for that,' she replied. 'I don't regret what I did. He deserved it.'

'Why did he deserve it?' asked Roscoe. 'For taking away your daughter?'

'Yes, for taking away my daughter,' said Cal, the anger instantly rising in her voice. 'And for locking me away for four years in an institution I should never have been in.'

'Why did Enzo bring you to London?'

'To play happy families. He thought I would pretend everything was fine, that I'd be grateful to be out. And that I'd do exactly what he wanted me to.'

'What did he want you to do?'

'To go to him again, to go to his suite, to his bed,' said Cal, the pain vibrating in her voice. 'Matteo told me at the airport in Chicago that he'd be here. That's why I ran away. I never thought I'd see him again, but when we arrived in London there he was, acting like one of the family. And I realised then Harper was in danger too.'

'Cal, who is Harper's father?' asked Roscoe.

She pressed her fingers into her eyes and smeared dirt-stained tears across her face.

'Uncle Oscar.'

CHAPTER 35

INSIDE THE WINDOWLESS POLICE interview room at New Scotland Yard, Roscoe threw back his chair and sprinted from the room.

As he ran down the hallway, Chief Inspector Fran Walker called after him, 'Roscoe, talk to me!'

But he was gone.

'Dad?' said Martin as Roscoe got into his SUV, fired the engine and accelerated away.

'Slight detour,' said Roscoe. 'We need to head back to the hotel before we go and see your sisters.'

'What's going on?'

'I knew there was something wrong when he approached me in the parking garage.'

'Who?'

'I think he was going to shoot me then.'

'Dad, look out!' exclaimed Martin as they flew through a red light.

Without touching his brakes, Roscoe swerved around a red London bus before he hit the accelerator again.

'I hope you're wearing your seatbelt,' he said, turning to Martin with a smile. 'Hit Anna's number on my phone.'

'I promise you I'm still doing fine,' said Anna, her voice on loudspeaker filling the car.

'Oscar Miller is the father of Harper Ginevra.'

'Miller?' said Anna, sounding shocked.

'Or "Uncle Oscar", as Cal called him,' said Roscoe. 'Miller worked together with Enzo Ginevra on the very first Tribeca Luxury Hotel. He became a fixture at the Ginevras' home, trusted by all. And he abused that trust in the sickest of ways.

'Cal gave birth to Miller's child and my guess is Enzo saw that as an opportunity to further his own interests. Either he decided to protect his business partner at the expense of his own daughter or, more likely, he chose to use Harper's birth to enhance his own empire. He had a hold over Miller and was ready to exploit it in every way possible. Ginevra Construction became the exclusive partner of Tribeca and the money flowed in. And that meant Matteo could become more and more reckless as he was simply untouchable.'

'Which ended in him killing two men in Chicago,' said Anna.

'And my guess is even that wasn't a problem because Uncle Oscar was despatched to take care of any potential witnesses.'

'Including you, Dad?' said Martin.

Roscoe turned to look at his son. 'I was the last man standing,' he said. 'I didn't realise at the time, but once I'd mentioned to Miller Cal having a child, he panicked. He came after me in the parking garage, but he lost his nerve and couldn't shoot me face to face. Instead he tried to shoot me through the bedroom door.'

CHAPTER 36

AS HE RACED THROUGH the gates of the Tribeca Luxury Hotel in Mayfair, Roscoe could see in his mirrors Chief Inspector Walker pursuing him in a police squad car. Accelerating up the driveway, he saw Oscar Miller sitting in the rear of a Tribeca limousine, waiting for his bags to be loaded into the trunk of the car.

Roscoe spun his SUV across the front of the limo, Martin gripping hold of his armrests as he did. The stench of burnt rubber hung in the air as Roscoe jumped from the car and ran to the limo.

Throwing open the rear door, he leant across the back seat as Miller sipped a glass of vintage champagne.

'Merry Christmas, Mr Miller.' He knocked the glass from Miller's hand, sending champagne flying across the car.

'What the hell . . . ?' said Miller. But Roscoe had already gripped the lapels of his grey cashmere coat and was dragging him head first out of the back of the limousine.

'You raped a child again and again!' he cried, throwing Miller against the side of the car. 'And you didn't feel one ounce of remorse!'

Roscoe's fist slammed against Miller's jaw before he dragged him to the front of the car. Pulling his head backwards, he prepared to slam Miller's face into the hood.

'No, Jon!' hollered Fran Walker, her car coming to a stop alongside Roscoe's. Jumping from the vehicle, she stood on the other side of Miller's car, imploring her former inspector. 'He isn't worth it.'

Roscoe looked at Walker, and then at Miller.

'You're never going to get that nasty bloodstain out of a nice coat like this,' he said, throwing Miller to the ground before two police officers quickly stepped forward and cuffed the man. 'But then again, I doubt you'll need it where you're headed.'

'You're going to make that shoulder even worse if you keep behaving like that,' said Anna as Roscoe walked through the towering glass door that led into the hotel's marbled foyer. She put her arms around him.

'Tell me you're okay,' said Roscoe.

'I'm not going to answer that question any more,' she replied with a smile. 'Will this change what happens to Cal?'

'She killed her father and she planned it. But a good barrister should make a strong defence. Let's hope there's a plea and it doesn't come to that.'

He looked back across the foyer to see Martin standing at the entrance to the hotel.

'You should go,' said Anna. 'You need to be with your family.'

'I might see you later?'

'I think I've earned my night off tonight,' she said as she kissed Roscoe on the cheek. 'I'll catch you tomorrow.'

CHAPTER 37

STANDING IN THE FRONT garden of her parents' home, Marika Roscoe heard a woman violently sobbing. Realising Emily Lee had been brought home that morning, she told her mother to take her daughters inside and she ran straight towards the neighbouring Montgomerie home.

As she entered the garden, the front door to the house opened, and Emily Lee crawled out on her hands and knees.

Marika could see her eye was blackened and her mouth split open.

Coming through the door after her, Wyatt grabbed hold of Emily's hair. Jerking her head backwards, he pulled her up onto her knees before spinning her around, back towards the house.

'Wyatt, please! I'm sorry,' she cried as he lifted her off the ground.

'Get back inside!' he yelled. 'How stupid did you think I am? You're the stupid one. Did you think you could steal my son? Tell me where you had him!'

Wyatt lurched at his wife and Marika saw her hopelessly try to clamber away.

'Kids don't just suddenly reappear!' he roared. 'Get back in the house!' His hand connected with his wife's face.

'Stop!' shouted Marika, making her way up the path. 'Stop it now, Wyatt!'

Wyatt turned to face her, and Marika realised he hadn't seen her until that moment. 'Get off this property,' he said in a disconcertingly calm tone.

'Not until you let her go.'

'Don't tell me what to do,' he replied, reaching down and gripping Emily by the hair again. Emily looked tragically at Marika, as though pleading with her to leave.

Marika couldn't do that.

'Wyatt, let Emily go,' she said.

Wyatt laughed. 'Do you think this is some kind of negotiation?' he said, moving towards Marika.

'Emily, I want you to go back inside the house, close the door and lock it behind you,' said Marika, issuing clear instructions in the hope of breaking her from her stupor.

Wyatt continued to walk towards Marika.

'Now!' shouted Marika, and Emily ran towards the front door.

Wyatt took three steps forward, wrapped his arm around Marika's neck and dragged her too towards the house. Seeing her husband's SUV pull up outside the house, Marika shouted for help.

But Wyatt was too strong. In a split second he had dragged her backwards into the house, kicked Emily through the door and forced Marika in after her.

Thrown to the floor, Marika stumbled down the hall as Wyatt Lee slammed the door closed behind them.

CHAPTER 38

ROSCOE SPRINTED DOWN THE path and with a single kick of his boot smashed through the front door of Dame Annabel's home.

Seeing Marika backing safely down the hallway, he turned to Emily, who sat cowering at the foot of the stairs, holding her young son Brayden.

With panic in his eyes, Wyatt went to grab the child. The boy screamed and clung defiantly to his mother. In one movement, Roscoe took hold of Wyatt by the back of his neck and hurled him through the open front door, which swung on its hinges.

Roscoe stepped out onto the path after him. Wyatt scrambled to his feet and started to run towards Roscoe's parked SUV. As he did the car door was thrown open, and with fantastic force it slammed like an iron fist into Lee's face, knocking him unconscious to the ground.

'Nice work,' said Roscoe, walking down the path.

'I didn't think that shoulder of yours could throw any more punches,' replied Martin with a smile. He stepped over his victim and made his way over to his dad.

CHAPTER 39

ROSCOE LOOKED ACROSS THE road to the small house at the side of the pond and wasn't surprised to see Julian Templeton peering through his window. Walking across the road, he saw a second figure slip away.

As he approached the house, the door was opened and Roscoe walked inside.

'Brayden has not been harmed in any way,' said Julian, following Roscoe into his living room.

'I know,' said Roscoe. 'Where is she?'

Julian turned his head to the kitchen door and raised his eyebrows. Roscoe stepped across and pushed the door open.

'It wasn't meant to be like this,' said Dame Annabel. She was leaning against a kitchen cabinet.

'Do you want to tell me how it was meant to be?' asked Roscoe.

'An intervention, she called it,' said Julian.

'Be quiet,' said Dame Annabel.

'I did everything you asked of me,' he continued. 'We'd rescue your grandson, you said, get your daughter out of a disastrous marriage. Nobody would get hurt, you said.'

'Julian!' snapped Dame Annabel. 'What you need to understand, Jon, is that my daughter, through no fault of her own, ended up in a violent and abusive marriage. I had to find a way to get her out of it.'

'So you kidnapped her son?' asked Roscoe.

'She would never leave Wyatt while he still had control of Brayden. He terrifies her, but she loves her son. I knew if I could get Brayden away it would end Wyatt's hold over her and give me a chance to persuade her to leave Wyatt.'

'But she ended up in hospital and it was impossible for you to talk to her?' said Roscoe.

'Exactly.'

'And I was left with the boy and very little gratitude for the danger I was suddenly facing,' said Julian.

'I shouldn't have put you in that position,' said Annabel.

'No, you should not,' said Julian. 'What excitement you said it would be. The first night you would stage the break-in, you said. If you hadn't guessed, Mr Roscoe, it was me who was responsible for the graffiti on the dame's car. And then, of course, late on Christmas Eve the boy was brought to me.'

'So when the alarm went off on Christmas morning . . .' said Roscoe.

'He was already safely hidden in the room beneath my kitchen.'

'It seems a stupid idea now,' said Dame Annabel, 'but I had to do something. You've seen how violent Wyatt can be.'

'I'm sure the police will have questions for you both.'

'Does it have to be that way, Jon? Brayden's safe and now surely Emily will see she has to escape from that man. I'm the only one who can help her do that.'

From outside the house Roscoe could hear police sirens approaching. 'Sounds to me as if it's already too late,' he said.

'Indeed it is,' said Julian with a satisfied smile. 'I've already made the call. I'm sorry, but you're no friend of mine, Dame Annabel.'

CHAPTER 40

ON THE THIRTY-NINTH FLOOR of the Tribeca Luxury Hotel in the Mayfair district of London was one of the finest Indian restaurants in the country. With views across the neighbouring royal park and beyond to the historic city, it was one of the most beautiful settings in the whole of the capital.

Reaching their table, Jon Roscoe pulled back his wife's chair before taking his seat opposite her.

'A memorable Christmas,' said Roscoe, touching his champagne glass against his wife's.

'You've saved me from seven years of bad luck for lying to my mother,' said Marika, looking across at him.

'I have?'

'I promised her we'd have dinner together before I left.'

'Hopefully not the worst promise to have to keep,' said Roscoe.

'You can't do any wrong in her eyes. And now she will dine out for a year on the story of how Dame Annabel enlisted the help of Julian Templeton to kidnap her own grandson.'

'Kind of crazy, keeping him hidden for two days in Julian's cellar,' said Roscoe.

'Misguided, certainly,' said Marika, taking a sip of champagne, 'but I saw what Wyatt Lee was capable of. If Dame Annabel was aware of half of that, I can understand exactly why she did it. Perhaps she went about it in the wrong way, but I think her heart was in the right place. She had to find a way to get her daughter and her grandson out of that marriage.'

'You're right,' said Roscoe. 'At the airport I thought Wyatt was genuinely reluctant to come to London but in reality he was taunting his wife, mocking her, finding another way to abuse her. I was so blinkered on Matteo Ginevra and Cal, I never realised it was Emily who had left me the note on the plane. Like Cal, she too was frightened for her life.'

'I wonder what Emily will do now.'

'Wyatt could be tried for assault, and my guess is the courts might look kindly on Dame Annabel and Julian. But perhaps Emily would be best making her own fresh start, just her and Brayden.' Roscoe paused as he looked across the restaurant.

Marika turned her head to look over her shoulder as a young Italian man, his jet-black hair slicked back, crossed the restaurant and approached their table. 'Who's that?' she said.

Roscoe scowled. 'That's Matteo Ginevra.'

'This must be the beautiful Mrs Roscoe,' said Ginevra as he held out his hand to Marika. 'Delighted to finally meet you.'

Roscoe clenched his fists and edged back in his chair.

'I'm sorry your family has had to endure such suffering,' replied Marika.

'Families like mine, Mrs Roscoe, live from generation to generation. We only grow stronger.'

Roscoe thought how much he detested the man. How was it that Cal, who had been so desperate to protect her daughter, was sitting in a police cell while Matteo, having killed two men, walked free?

'I'll leave you to enjoy your meal, Mrs Roscoe,' said Ginevra. 'I've an early flight back to Chicago in the morning.'

Roscoe watched as he walked away and out of the restaurant. Oscar Miller may have been about to be charged but Ginevra was the man Roscoe wanted to see convicted.

'You have to let it go, Jon,' said Marika, reaching for her husband's hand.

'I never will,' he replied. 'That man is evil and causes suffering wherever he goes.'

'That's what makes me afraid. You have to walk away and be ready to put me and the girls first.'

'Walk away from a man I know is guilty?' Roscoe rubbed his eyes. 'I'm sorry, Marika, I can't do that.'

'Then however much I love you, I can't live like that,' said Marika, pulling her hand away. 'I think it's time for me to go home.'

Have yourself a scary little Christmas

STORIES AT THE SPEED OF LIFE

JAMES
PATTERSON
BOOKSHOTS

A high-society murder.
Stolen priceless paintings.
Christmas will be no
holiday for Detective
Luc Moncrief.

THE
CHRISTMAS
MYSTERY

WITH RICHARD DILALLO

Read on for an extract

PROLOGUE

CHAOS AND CONFUSION reign in New York City's most glamorous department store, Bloomingdale's.

A dozen beautiful women—perfect makeup, perfect clothing—are strutting around the first floor, armed. No one escapes these women. They are shooting customers…with spritzes of expensive perfume.

Enough fragrance fills the air to create a lethal cloud of nausea. The effect is somewhere between expensive flower shop and cheap brothel.

"Unbelievable! This place is packed," says K. Burke.

"Yes," I say. "You'd think it was almost Christmas."

"It *is* almost Chris—" Burke begins to say. She stops, then adds, "Don't be a wiseass, Moncrief. We've got a long day ahead of us."

K. Burke and I are police detective partners from Manhattan's Midtown East. Our chief inspector, Nick Elliott, has assigned us to undercover security at this famous and glamorous department store. I told the inspector that I preferred more challenging assignments, "like trapping terrorists and capturing murderers."

Elliott's response?

"Feel free to trap any terrorists or capture any murderers you come across. Meanwhile, keep your eyes open for purse-snatchers and shoplifters."

K. Burke, ever the cooperative pro, said, "I understand, sir."

I said nothing.

In any event, K. Burke and I at this moment are standing in a fog of Caron Poivre and Chanel No. 5 in Bloomingdale's perfume department.

"So, how are we going to split up, Moncrief?" asks Burke.

"You decide," I say. My enthusiasm is not overwhelming.

"Okay," Burke says. "I'll take the second floor…women's designer clothes. Why don't you take high-end gifts? China, crystal, silver."

"May I suggest," I say, "that you take women's designer clothing on the *fourth* floor, not the *second*. Second floor is Donna Karan and Calvin. Fourth floor is Dolce & Gabbana, Prada, Valentino. Much classier."

Burke shakes her head. "It's amazing, the stuff you know."

We test-check the red buttons on our cell phones, the communication keys that give us immediate contact with each other.

Burke says that she'll also notify regular store security and tell them that their special request NYPD patrol is there, as planned.

"I've got to get out of this perfume storm," she says. She's just about to move toward the central escalator when a well-dressed middle-aged woman approaches. The woman speaks directly to Burke.

"Where can I buy one of these?" the woman says.

"I got the last one," Burke says. The woman laughs and walks away.

I'm completely confused. "What was that lady asking about?" I say.

"She was asking about you," Burke says. "As if you didn't know." Burke walks quickly toward the up escalator.

WITHIN THREE MINUTES I'm standing in the Fine China and Silver section of Bloomingdale's sixth floor. If there is a problem with the economy in New York City, someone failed to tell the frantic shoppers snapping up Wedgwood soup tureens and sterling silver dinner forks. It's only ten thirty in the morning, yet the line at gift-wrap is already eight customers deep.

My cell phone is connected to hundreds of store security cameras. These cameras are trained on entrance areas, exit doors, credit card registers—all areas where intruders can enter, exit, and operate quickly.

I keep my head still, but my eyes dart around the area. Like Christmas itself, all is calm, all is bright. I make my way through the crowd of wealthy-looking women in fur, prosperous-looking men with five-hundred-dollar cashmere scarves.

Then a loud buzz. Insistent. Urgent. I glance quickly at my phone. The red light. I listen to K. Burke's voice.

"Second floor. Right now," she says. She immediately clicks off.

Damn it. I told her to go to the fourth floor. Burke makes her own decisions.

Within a few seconds I'm at the Bloomingdale's internal staircase. I skip the stairs three at a time. I burst through the second floor door.

Chaos. Screaming. Customers crowding the aisles near the down escalators. Salespeople crouched behind counters.

"Location Monitor" on my cell notifies me that Burke is no longer on the original second floor location. Her new location is men's furnishings—ties, wallets, aftershave. Ground floor.

I reverse my course and rush toward the rear escalator near Third Avenue. I push a few men and women out of my path. Now I'm struggling to execute a classic crazy move—I'm running *down* an escalator that's running *up*.

I land on the floor. I see K. Burke moving quickly past display cases of sweaters and shirts. Burke sees me.

She shouts one word.

"Punks!"

It's a perfect description. In a split second I see two young women—teens probably, both in dark-gray hoodies. The pair open a door marked EMPLOYEES ONLY. They go through. The door closes behind them.

Burke and I almost collide at that door. We know from our surveillance planning that this is one of Bloomingdale's "snare" closets—purposely mismarked to snare shoplifters and muggers on the run. This time it works like a Christmas charm. We enter the small space and see two tough-looking teenage girls—nose piercings, eyebrow piercings, tats, the whole getup. One of them is holding an opened switchblade. I squeeze her wrist between my thumb and index finger. The knife falls to the ground. As K. Burke scoops up the knife, she speaks.

"These two assholes knocked over a woman old enough to be their grandmother and took off with her shopping bag," Burke says. "They also managed to slash her leg—the long way. EMU is taking care of her."

"It ain't us. You're messed up. Look. No shopping bags," one of the girls says. Her voice is arrogant, angry.

"Store security has the shopping bag. And they've got enough video on the two of you to make a feature film," Burke adds.

It's clear to the young thieves that they'll get no place good with Burke. One of them decides to play me.

"Give us a break, man. It probably isn't even us on the video. I know all about this shit. Come on."

I smile at the young lady.

"You know all about this shit? Let me tell you something." I pause for a moment, then continue quietly. "In some cases, with the holidays approaching, I might say: give the kids a warning and release them."

"That'd be way cool," says her friend.

K. Burke looks at me. I know that she's afraid my liberal soft spot is going to erupt.

"But this is not one of those cases," I say.

"Man, no. Why?" asks the girl.

"I believe my colleague summed it up a few minutes ago," I say.

"What the hell?" the girl says.

I answer. "Punks!"

THE CHRISTMAS MYSTERY

Almost Thanksgiving

WHEN DALIA BOAZ died a few months ago, I believed that my own life had ended along with hers.

Friends suggested that, with time, the agony of the loss would diminish.

They were wrong. Day after day I ache for Dalia, the love of my life. Yet life rattles on. Unstoppable. Yes, there are moments when I am joyful. Other times are inevitably heartbreaking: Dalia's birthday, my birthday, the anniversary of a special romantic event. Holidays are a special problem, of course, because I am surrounded by celebration—Easter baskets overflowing, fireworks erupting, bright lights hanging from evergreen trees.

Thanksgiving Day is a unique problem. There is nothing remotely like it in France. When Dalia was alive, if I was not on duty, we stayed in bed and streamed a few movies, whipped up some omelets, topped them with beluga caviar, and were thankful that we did not have to eat sweet potatoes with melted marshmallows.

This Thanksgiving proved a challenge. A few detective colleagues generously and sincerely invited me to join them. No, that wasn't for me. So I volunteered for holiday assignment. But

Inspector Elliott informed me that Thanksgiving was well-staffed with both detectives and officers (mostly divorced parents who traded seeing their children on Thanksgiving Day for seeing them on Christmas Day).

For a moment I wondered how my partner would be spending her holiday. Although my knowledge of K. Burke's private life was sparse, I knew that both her parents were deceased.

Casually I asked her, "Where are you going for Thanksgiving?"

"The gym," was her answer.

In an unlikely explosion of sentiment that surprised even myself I said, "Come to my place. I'll fix Thanksgiving dinner for both of us."

"Yeah, sure," was her sarcastic reaction. "And I'll bake a pumpkin pie."

"No. I'm serious."

"You are?" she said, trying to hide her surprise.

With only a hint of confusion she spoke slowly and quietly. "Oh, my God. This feels like a date."

"I assure you, it is not," I said.

Both Burke and I knew that I meant it.

Then I added, "But please do *not* bake a pumpkin pie."

Thanksgiving

"THIS PLACE IS...well, it's sort of unbelievable," K. Burke says. She stands in the entrance gallery to my new apartment and spreads her arms in amazement.

"Merci," I say. "I had to find a new home after Dalia died. I could not stay in her place. I could not stay in mine. Too many..." I pause.

Detective Burke nods. Of course, she knows. Too many memories. I take her on a brief tour of the place. A loft on Madison Square, a single three-thousand-foot room with a view of the Flatiron Building to the south and the Empire State Building to the north. The huge room is sparse—purposely so. Steel furniture, glass side tables, black-and-white Cartier-Bresson photographs of Paris.

We eventually move to the table for Thanksgiving dinner. The small black lacquered table is set with my great-grandmother's vintage Limoges.

As we begin the main course of the dinner, K. Burke says, "The only thing more impressive than this apartment is this meal."

Another *Merci.*

"Moncrief, I've known you almost a year. I've spent hundreds of hours with you. I've been on a police case in Europe with you. I…I never knew you could cook like this. I just can't believe you can make a meal like this."

"Well, K. Burke. I *cannot* make a meal like this. But fortunately Steve Miller, the senior sous-chef at Gramercy Tavern, was happy to make such a meal."

And what a feast it is.

Burke and I begin with a truffled chestnut soup. Then, instead of a big bird plopped in the middle of the table, Miller has layered thin slices of turkey breast in a creamy sauce of Gruyère cheese and porcini mushrooms. Instead of the dreaded sweet potatoes, we are dining on crisp pommes frites and a delicious cool salad, a combination of shredded brussels sprouts and pomegranate seeds.

"This is what the food in heaven tastes like," K. Burke says.

"No, this is what the food in Gramercy Tavern tastes like."

I pour us each some wine. We clink glasses.

"What shall we toast to?" she says.

I say, "Let us toast to a good friendship during a difficult year."

She hesitates just for a moment. Then K. Burke says, "Yes. To a good friendship."

We drink.

She holds up her glass again.

"One more thing I want to toast to," Burke says.

"Yes?" I say, hoping it will not be sentimental, hoping it will not be about Dalia, hoping…

"Let's toast to you and me really trying to see eye to eye from now on."

"Excellent idea," I say. We clink glasses again. We begin to devour the wonderful food.

And then her cell phone rings. Burke quickly puts down her fork and slips the phone out of her pocket. She reads the name.

"It's Inspector Elliott."

"Don't answer it," I say.

"We've got to answer it, Moncrief."

"Don't answer it," I repeat. "*We* are having dinner."

"*You* are a lunatic," she says.

I roll my eyes and speak.

"So much for trying to see eye to eye."

OF COURSE, K. BURKE triumphs. She takes Inspector Elliott's call.

Fifteen minutes later we're in the detective squad room of Midtown East watching Elliott eat a slice of pie. K. Burke later tells me that it is filled with something called mincemeat, made out of beef fat and brandy. *Incroyable!*

"This could have waited until tomorrow, but you both told me that you wanted to work today. So I assumed you'd be free," Elliott says.

Then he looks us both up and down closely, Burke in a simple, elegant gray skirt with a black shirt; me in a navy blue Brioni bespoke suit.

"But you both are dressed like you've just come from the White House."

Neither Burke nor I speak. We are certainly not going to tell our boss where we were dining fifteen minutes earlier.

"In any event, I decided to come in and do some desk work. My wife packed me some pie. And I figured I could watch Green Bay kick the Bears' ass on my iPad instead of watching it on TV with my brother-in-law."

Then he gets down to business.

"I thought this problem might go away, but it's real. Very real. Potentially dangerous. And it involves some New York City big shots."

Elliott swallows the last chunk of his pie. Then he continues speaking. He's energetic, anxious. Whatever it is, it's going to be a big deal.

"You two ever heard of the Namanworth Gallery up on 57th Street?"

"I think so," says Burke. "Just off Park Avenue."

"That's the one," says Elliott. "You know the place, Moncrief? It sounds like something you'd be down with."

"As a matter of fact, I *do* know that gallery. They handled the sale of a Kandinsky to a friend of mine a few months ago, and a few years back my father was talking to them about a Rothko. Nothing came of it."

"Well, your dad might have lucked out," says Elliott. "We've got some pretty heavy evidence that they've been dealing in the most impeccable forgeries in New York. A lot of collectors have been screwed over by them."

I speak.

"Namanworth hasn't owned that place for thirty years. A husband and wife are the owners. Sophia and Andre Krane. I think she claims to have been a countess or duchess or something."

"We don't know about her royal blood. But we do know that Barney Wexler, the guy who owns that cosmetics company, paid them thirty-five million dollars for a Klimt painting. And he thinks it was…"

I finish his sentence for him. "...not painted by Klimt."

Elliott says, "And Wexler's lined up two experts who can back him up."

"Although the case sounds really exciting..." Burke says, "there's a special division for art-and-antique counterfeit work."

"Yeah," says Elliott. "But with these big players, there may be more to it than simple forgery. Where there's smoke, there's usually fire. And where there's valuable artwork, there's possible fraud, possible money-laundering—ultimately, possible homicides. So they want us to stick our dirty noses in it. We can call on counterfeit if we want."

I speak. "I don't think we'll want to do that."

"That's what I thought you'd say, Moncrief." Then he taps a button on his computer. "There, I've just sent you all the info on the case. You'll see. It's not just Wexler. These are the money-men *and* the money-women who rock this town.

"By the way, there's a special pain in the ass about this case...."

"Isn't there always?" Burke says.

"This is particularly painful," says Elliott. "The Kranes aren't talking. They're comfy in their eight-hundred-acre Catskills estate."

"The hell with that," says Burke. "We'll get an order from justice."

"No, you won't, not when the attorney general of the state of New York says they don't have to cooperate."

"What the hell is that all about?" I say.

"Exactly," says Elliott. "What the hell is that all about?"

JAMES PATTERSON
BOOK**SHOTS**
OUT THIS MONTH

THE CHRISTMAS MYSTERY

Two priceless paintings disappear from a Park Avenue
murder scene – French detective Luc Moncrief is in
for a not-so-merry Christmas.

COME AND GET US

Miranda Cooper's life takes a terrifying turn when an SUV deliberately
runs her and her husband off a desolate Arizona road.

RADIANT: THE DIAMOND
TRILOGY, PART 2

Siobhan has moved to Detroit following her traumatic break-up
with Derick, but when Derick comes after her, Siobhan
must decide whether she can trust him again . . .

HOT WINTER NIGHTS

Allie Fairchild made a mistake when she moved to Montana,
but just when she's about to throw in the towel, life in
Bear Mountain takes a surprisingly sexy turn . . .

ALSO BY JAMES PATTERSON

ALEX CROSS NOVELS
Along Came a Spider
Kiss the Girls
Jack and Jill
Cat and Mouse
Pop Goes the Weasel
Roses are Red
Violets are Blue
Four Blind Mice
The Big Bad Wolf
London Bridges
Mary, Mary
Cross
Double Cross
Cross Country
Alex Cross's Trial (*with Richard DiLallo*)
I, Alex Cross
Cross Fire
Kill Alex Cross
Merry Christmas, Alex Cross
Alex Cross, Run
Cross My Heart
Hope to Die
Cross Justice
Cross the Line

THE WOMEN'S MURDER CLUB SERIES
1st to Die
2nd Chance (*with Andrew Gross*)
3rd Degree (*with Andrew Gross*)
4th of July (*with Maxine Paetro*)
The 5th Horseman (*with Maxine Paetro*)

The 6th Target (*with Maxine Paetro*)
7th Heaven (*with Maxine Paetro*)
8th Confession (*with Maxine Paetro*)
9th Judgement (*with Maxine Paetro*)
10th Anniversary (*with Maxine Paetro*)
11th Hour (*with Maxine Paetro*)
12th of Never (*with Maxine Paetro*)
Unlucky 13 (*with Maxine Paetro*)
14th Deadly Sin (*with Maxine Paetro*)
15th Affair (*with Maxine Paetro*)

DETECTIVE MICHAEL BENNETT SERIES
Step on a Crack (*with Michael Ledwidge*)
Run for Your Life (*with Michael Ledwidge*)
Worst Case (*with Michael Ledwidge*)
Tick Tock (*with Michael Ledwidge*)
I, Michael Bennett (*with Michael Ledwidge*)
Gone (*with Michael Ledwidge*)
Burn (*with Michael Ledwidge*)
Alert (*with Michael Ledwidge*)
Bullseye (*with Michael Ledwidge*)

PRIVATE NOVELS
Private (*with Maxine Paetro*)
Private London (*with Mark Pearson*)
Private Games (*with Mark Sullivan*)
Private: No. 1 Suspect (*with Maxine Paetro*)
Private Berlin (*with Mark Sullivan*)

Private Down Under (*with Michael White*)

Private L.A. (*with Mark Sullivan*)

Private India (*with Ashwin Sanghi*)

Private Vegas (*with Maxine Paetro*)

Private Sydney (*with Kathryn Fox*)

Private Paris (*with Mark Sullivan*)

The Games (*with Mark Sullivan*)

NYPD RED SERIES

NYPD Red (*with Marshall Karp*)

NYPD Red 2 (*with Marshall Karp*)

NYPD Red 3 (*with Marshall Karp*)

NYPD Red 4 (*with Marshall Karp*)

STAND-ALONE THRILLERS

Sail (*with Howard Roughan*)

Swimsuit (*with Maxine Paetro*)

Don't Blink (*with Howard Roughan*)

Postcard Killers (*with Liza Marklund*)

Toys (*with Neil McMahon*)

Now You See Her (*with Michael Ledwidge*)

Kill Me If You Can (*with Marshall Karp*)

Guilty Wives (*with David Ellis*)

Zoo (*with Michael Ledwidge*)

Second Honeymoon (*with Howard Roughan*)

Mistress (*with David Ellis*)

Invisible (*with David Ellis*)

The Thomas Berryman Number

Truth or Die (*with Howard Roughan*)

Murder House (*with David Ellis*)

Never Never (*with Candice Fox*)

Woman of God (*with Maxine Paetro*)

BOOKSHOTS

Black & Blue (*with Candice Fox*)

Break Point (*with Lee Stone*)

Cross Kill

Private Royals (*with Rees Jones*)

The Hostage (*with Robert Gold*)

Zoo 2 (*with Max DiLallo*)

Heist (*with Rees Jones*)

Hunted (*with Andrew Holmes*)

Airport: Code Red (*with Michael White*)

The Trial (*with Maxine Paetro*)

Little Black Dress (*with Emily Raymond*)

Chase (*with Michael Ledwidge*)

Let's Play Make-Believe (*with James O. Born*)

Dead Heat (*with Lee Stone*)

Triple Threat

113 Minutes (*with Max DiLallo*)

The Verdict (*with Robert Gold*)

French Kiss (*with Richard DiLallo*)

$10,000,000 Marriage Proposal (*with Hilary Liftin*)

Kill or Be Killed

Taking the Titanic (*with Scott Slaven*)

Killer Chef (*with Jeffrey J. Keyes*)